I Am a
Caregiver

a love story

Michelle Bailey, M.A

"There are only four kinds of people in the world: those who have been caregivers, those who are currently caregivers, those who will be caregivers, and those who will need caregivers."

Rosalynn Carter

Dedication

I dedicate this book to all the caregivers out there who think they are unseen, underpaid and undervalued. I see you. You are not alone!

I would also like to dedicate this book to my husband, Bill, who taught us all how to value life, live it to the fullest and showed us how to make the most out of every situation, no matter how painful or uncomfortable.

Acknowledgment

I'd like to thank my friend and neighbor, Pam, for always being there for me and providing critical insight to patients with Alzheimer's.

But most of all, I want to thank our family for their constant love and support, which helped us survive the toughest of times, and for my son and daughter who unselfishly gave their time to improve the quality of life for their father.

A Glimpse into Life Behind the Words

Shelly Bailey shares a raw and heart-wrenching look at the last 10 years as a caregiver for her husband of 48 years. Her story is deeply personal, yet lovingly resilient as she gives the reader a hard and realistic look at what caregiving actually entails. Although educated in Behavioral Science and Human Behavior, nothing prepared her for the harsh realities of caring for someone whose debilitating disease left them completely dependent on her, and how woefully unprepared she was to take on that responsibility financially, physically, and emotionally. Yet, love endures, and attitude is indeed everything.

Early Life and Inspiration

Not unknown to publication, she is launching her first autobiographical book and the release of two children's books she wrote and illustrated for her grandchildren, Hobie and ZuZu, while caring for her bedridden husband. Prior to that, while pursuing her graduate degree, she co-authored a research-based article with Dr. Robert Epstein in Psychology Today on the work of Dr. B.F. Skinner and his acclaimed and controversial experiments with Air cribs, or Baby Boxes, as it was also referred to.

This book, however, spans a lifetime of caregiving not just on a personal level, but professionally, as she sought careers in the helping professions. Whether helping people find careers, designing plans for creating housing communities for the unhoused, or approving funding applications for low-income and supportive housing, her passion for helping her community went hand-in-hand with caring for her family.

Legacy and Vision

This book offers hope and a vision for a call to action, not only for the baby-boomer generation, but for the next generations that will no doubt face the same dilemma when caring for loved ones. The same questions we will all ask when facing the gut-wrenching decisions of what to do with a loved one who needs care. Who is going to care for them? How much is it going to cost? And where is that money coming from?

Shelly is a mother to two grown children and Nonna to a granddaughter and two grandsons. She lived and worked in San Diego for most of her life, but currently resides in Northern California, where she has lived and worked for over 15 years. Among her many interests, rockhounding prompted her to set up a lapidary shop in her garage. She turned semi-precious stones she found into cabochons and has made a line of jewelry she plans to post on an Etsy site under the name

Michelle Channels Designs (her mother's birth name). She still has plans to keep writing.

Table of Contents

Introduction

I am and have always been a caregiver. I say that because I now know it is in my nature to be a caregiver, and when I look back at my life, I realize it has been my primary role. Whether as a child, teenager, or adult, I have always been a caregiver. So, it seemed only natural to write about caregiving. Even as a child, in an alcoholic household, I was tasked with looking after my brother and sister, as I was the eldest of three. When they were kicked out of our parents' home, I took them into my husband's and mine's home as young adults to help them get their feet back on the ground. There was never a point in my life where I wouldn't bend over backwards to help my family, never a doubt, never a question. I would help them in any way I could. That is what a caregiver does. Little did I know I would be put to the test in a way I could have never imagined.

I now consider myself somewhat of a caregiving expert. My expertise of late comes from having cared for my bedridden husband for the last 10 years. My decision to write this book stems from the lessons I've learned along the way in hopes I can help others navigate the tumultuous and challenging journey of caregiving and come out the other side unscathed. I now realize that is not realistic. However, there is hope and resources available to aid you as you make your way through the trials and tribulations along the way.

When I started this book, I wanted to give the reader experiences they could relate to without bombarding them with too much information. I wanted to tell my story while providing tools and resources I wish I had had from the beginning. I certainly didn't want this to be another self-help book. However, I soon realized that there were aspects of this book that took on those qualities. The jury is still out on whether or not self-help books are actually helpful.

My hope when reading this book is not to compare my experience to other more dramatic or horrific experiences, (I'm quite certain they're out there) but rather, to look through the pain, sadness and anger, and see that no matter how hopeless or invisible you may feel, there is hope and with hope, we find an inner strength we never knew we had. I know without a shadow of a doubt that I am stronger today as a result of these experiences. In an ocean of negative thoughts and feelings, that is a positive I'd like the reader to take away from this book.

I also felt it necessary to point out the misuse of hurtful cliches, or negative phrases such as *"There's always someone worse off!"* or *"Have you tried…?"* You know, people who are always wanting to help you and are sure there is something you missed. They are coming from a place of love and concern, but it's hard to see that when you think you've tried everything. As a caregiver, I'm sure you've heard these phrases and more. But in my research, I also found many quotes and phrases that were comforting and somewhat uplifting, so I included some of the ones I found particularly appropriate and helpful, such as *"Be patient and tough; someday this pain will be useful to you."* Ovid or *"Only great pain is the ultimate liberator of the spirit."* Friedrich Nietzsche, under resources at the end of the book. Apparently, there are some positive things that can come from pain. I'll let you be the judge.

There are, however, some phrases we never hope to hear as we go through difficult times. A good friend of mine, who has a husband with Alzheimer's, once told me that if she heard someone tell her to *"Hang in there"* one more time, she would scream. I knew exactly what she meant. There are plenty of negative phrases that probably hurt or angered you. I am particularly sensitive to phrases like: *"It's mind over matter,"* or *"Does that condition really exist?"* or my favorite, *"Maybe if they lost some weight…"* Having gone through this caregiving journey, I have become more sensitive and empathetic toward people going through pain or trauma of any kind. There is a right and a wrong way of comforting someone going through a painful experience. Let's face it, wouldn't you rather hear, *"I'm so sorry this has happened to you"* than *"I feel so sorry for you"*? One evokes pity, the other empathy.

As uncomfortable as some of my experiences may be, I will share my honest, raw, and candid thoughts and feelings while having gone through them, in the hope that you can relate on some level and not feel like you're the only one going through this. You're not…there are so many of us out there, and we are all but ignored, taken for granted, unseen, undervalued, underpaid, or not paid at all, and perhaps most of all, isolated from society.

For those of you who have sought to find help, you know how expensive and how hard it is to find good caregivers. Many health plans don't cover caregiving, and neither does Medicare. If you are in a lower income bracket, you may qualify for Medical or Medicaid[1]. To my knowledge, that is the only government assistance you can receive for caregiving. And if you are one of the smart ones who had the resources and thought ahead of time about getting long-term health care insurance, good on you! But you probably also learned how expensive long-term health care coverage actually is. Several variables come into play when determining the annual costs for long-term health care insurance, ranging from hundreds of dollars annually to thousands.

One must also consider the kind of coverage needed (e.g. skilled nursing, assisted living, in-home care, or convalescent care). The more coverage you get, the higher the premiums.

There are resources out there, I know, because I received somewhere in the neighborhood of $9,500 in respite grants over the last eight years from an organization that distributes funding to caregiving organizations who, in turn, provide respite to caregivers and

------

[1] $1 Trillion Medicaid funding cuts over 10 years made through Megabill passage-2025

their families. This really saved me as I was able to get away for four or more hours at a time, and that gave me a chance to recharge. I've come to believe that, no matter what your situation, you need to get away, if for no other reason than for your own sanity. Caregiver burnout is a real thing, and the stats out there do not favor caregivers. In fact, there are some very alarming statistics that really made me take a hard look at what I am doing and the impact it's having on my psyche and physical well-being.

The primary reason this topic is getting so much attention now is because the need for caregivers is increasing as the Baby Boomer generation ages out, and the husbands, wives, daughters, sons, sisters, and brothers are left to care for their loved ones as they get older or become ill, and are unable to care for themselves. This is evidenced in much of the research I found. A team of researchers at A Place For Mom, a non-profit caregiving organization, analyzed the latest caregiver demographics, and here's what they found:

- In 2020, 41.8 million Americans provided unpaid care to an adult over the age of 50. That's nearly 17% of the U.S. adult population.
- 89% of caregivers provide care for a relative or other loved one, such as a spouse.
- 23.7 hours per week is the average amount of time caregivers spend providing unpaid care for loved ones they don't live with; those who live with their care recipient spend 37.4 hours a week.
- More than 75% of all caregivers are female.

- The average caregiver is 50.1 years old.
- Caregivers provide an estimated $470 billion in free labor each year.

As troubling as those statistics may be, the one stat that bothered me the most is the one study that indicated 70% of all caregivers over the age of 70 die first[2]. They refer to this condition as Caregiver's Syndrome, which is "a debilitating condition brought on by unrelieved, constant caring for a person with a chronic illness or dementia."[3] So by labeling it as a Syndrome, you'd think that might lend it some credibility in the medical field or at least draw the attention of lobbyists or grassroots organizations that promote financial assistance and resources for caregivers. Yet, as scarce as that level of help may be, I did find some legislative bills on the docket that looked hopeful. I encourage you to check them out and advocate for those that make sense to you.

The California Coalition on Family Caregiving reviewed proposed state policies at the beginning of the year (2023) and voted on two priority policies to champion this legislative cycle: AB 518 and SB 616. The selection was based on which policies would have "the highest impact on family caregivers' well-being."[4] In October 2023, Governor

---

[2] Barron, Rosenberg, Mayoras & Mayoras P.C.September 15, 2014

[3] J. Posner, Health, November 2014

[4] The California Coalition on Family Caregiving, May, 31, 2023

Gavin Newsom signed SB 616 by Senator Lena Gonzales (D-Long Beach), guaranteeing workers at least five paid sick days per year, up from the current three days, while also increasing the accrual and carryover amounts. AB 518 would expand eligibility for benefits under the Paid Family Leave program to include individuals who take time off work to care for a seriously ill designated person. The bill defines a "designated person" as any individual related by blood or whose association with the employee is the equivalent of a family relationship. The bill would authorize the employee to identify the designated person when they file a claim for benefits. The bill would make conforming changes to the definitions of the terms "family care leave" and "family member." The California Coalition on Family Caregiving supports AB 518 so that paid family leave is accessible for all caregiving relationships. Status: The amended version of this bill was enacted in July 2024.

Additionally, the coalition voted to support 12 pieces of legislation that "impact family caregivers and/or care recipients." The coalition has expressed this support by submitting letters and stating support in person or over the phone at legislative committee hearings. For a complete list of pending legislation, please look at the end of the book under legislation.

This is a good start, but so much more is needed. I would love to see Medicare cover some or all of the cost of hiring professional caregivers, or incentives and tax breaks for full-time, in-home, unpaid caregivers. If I had the time and the energy actually to follow caregiver legislation, I would gladly advocate for these bills and perhaps champion more. For now, I will be satisfied telling my story, if for no other reason than for therapeutic self-preservation and to help others in my position.

Finally, and most importantly, I want to convey that love was the motivating factor in all the decisions I made. A love that endured for 50 years. A love that made what could have been a short and painful end, a long and happy story that held a family together like glue, which gave our grandchildren a chance to get to know their poppa, and would last for generations to come.

Part I:

Before the Fall

Chapter 1: The Night that Changed Our Lives Forever

On a moonless night, after a wonderful dinner in Cedar Breaks, we slowly made our way back to our RV. All the signs along the narrow two-lane highway only served to remind us of what we already knew. "Deer Crossing" was a common occurrence, most residents were aware of and knew better not to drive on this particular highway at night. We didn't have much of a choice as everything was closed in the winter, including Lake Panguitch Resort, which my husband was so anxious to show me, predicated on the fond memories of the many work trips there to experience some of the best fresh lake fishing anywhere. One of the many perks of the company he worked for. Disappointed, we were forced to go to the next closest town for dinner, which turned out to be Cedar Breaks.

Bellies full and feeling satiated, we were still keenly aware of the glowing eyes on both sides of the road. It was approximately 13 miles from Lake Panguitch campground to Cedar Breaks, but we took our time driving back, knowing deer crossing was something we needed to watch out for. I was responsible for checking on both sides of the highway, while my husband crawled along at 30 miles an hour. The pitch black night would only be illuminated by vehicles coming in the opposite direction, which made it harder to see anything attempting to cross the road, but we were confident, as it seemed we were the only ones driving on the road at that late hour.

Only a few short miles from our campsite, a glow up ahead signaled an approaching vehicle. As the car approached, we were temporarily blinded, and just as it passed us, the unthinkable happened: a deer jumped right out in front of us before we even knew what happened. It was as if the deer knew the exact moment it needed to cross in order to ensure immediate death.

There was no hope of avoiding it. Now I understand the meaning of "A deer in the headlights." The deer and I locked eyes for a millisecond, not knowing that our lives would be forever changed.

The jolt was minimal, but we freaked out, not expecting that to happen. The thud against our jeep left no doubt that the deer would be severely wounded or dead. My husband got out and confirmed the demise of the poor deer and assessed the damage to the front of our jeep. Being an animal lover, I was extremely upset that we had killed a deer, more so than any damage our jeep incurred. We were in a state of disbelief. We had tried so hard to avoid that very thing from happening, and BAM! Out of freakin' nowhere!

Even though we were on the last leg of our trip, it didn't preclude making touristy stops along the way back home. But this incident left no doubt that we were going straight home. Worse yet, we had to limp home, not knowing the extent of damage to our jeep and knowing we were going to have to have it repaired before we could even think about another trip.

My husband and I were fine, other than the utter shock and dismay of actually hitting a deer. We certainly had a story to tell, which we capitalized on at every opportunity. Our beautiful beetle-wing green jeep was back after getting a new grill, and we would be back on the road and to our wonderful, carefree RV life in no time. Or so we thought…

My husband's symptoms started slowly, with slight discomfort and strange sensations in his lower intestines and core, which prompted a myriad of tests that were inconclusive. In other words, they had no clue what was going on. A couple of months went by, and it became increasingly apparent that something serious was going on. My husband complained of numbness in his lower extremities, his breathing became labored, and his ability to walk became slow and lethargic. No one could figure out what was going on until the morning, like any other morning, he attempted to get out of bed. His legs were gone. Unable to get him in the jeep myself, I called my son and brother-in-law to help me get him to the ER.

Numerous tests, CT Scan, and ER physician visits later, the hospital resident Neurosurgeon came in with the grim news… "the casing around your spinal cord has been severely pinched, leaving a thread-like connection, and the nerve endings in your extremities have been compromised, rendering you all but paralyzed. You will probably not make it through the weekend." He told us to go home and get our things in order because my husband was going to die, as there was nothing more they could do. *My husband was going to die!!!???* In utter disbelief, it took a few agonizing seconds to realize what he just said. *How could that be possible? Why couldn't they do anything for him? What was happening?* My otherwise calm demeanor suddenly erupted in a series of racking sobs and questions, all with the same inevitable ending.

My husband and I sat stunned, looking at each other in total disbelief. I crumbled and cried, even though something inside me still couldn't believe it. My husband, being the logical, pragmatic person he was, made the impossible phone calls to family, informing them he had a couple of days before he became completely paralyzed, resulting in cardiac or respiratory arrest and death, while I sat at his bedside with my head in my hands, sobbing uncontrollably. At some point, a phone call was made to his general practitioner to get some perspective on the fatal diagnosis we had just received, and he made the recommendation that saved my husband's life. He referred us to a very well-known and prominent Neurosurgeon. Given the urgency of the situation, we were able to get him an appointment the next day.

The doctor took one look at the CT Scan image and canceled all his next-day appointments. Emergency surgery took place the following morning. The surgery would not be easy; in fact, it was considered extremely risky, which is why the ER doctor would have nothing to do with it. As difficult as it was, it would not cure him; it would only save his life, and he would be restored to his current state, which was already extremely limited. The decision was easy: to save his life. We would deal with the aftermath later. This would prove to be the most challenging time in our lives.

The surgery would take six hours, give or take an hour based on any complications. The procedure involved scraping bone on six vertebrae, starting at the base of his neck and extending almost to the center of his back. This would remove the pressure being applied to the spinal cord and restore some feeling to his extremities, but only on a limited basis, as the bone had practically closed the spinal column completely. There was no way to know for sure how much movement he would actually have. Rehabilitation and physical therapy would be a key part of recovery. That is what we were told. That is what we believed.

I remember walking into my husband's hospital room right after surgery and seeing this huge bandage and brace around his neck, and the look on his face told me he was in excruciating pain. Horrified, I quickly walked out of his room to prevent him from seeing me and my daughter, who came with me, from breaking down. According to the doctor, the surgery went well. No complications; however, he had to spend 36 hours in the ICU. After that, it was a waiting game. We really wouldn't know the extent of his ability to move his extremities for at least a couple of days. In the meantime, he really didn't want visitors—he didn't want anyone to see him like that.

When it came time to test his movement, he was able to move both arms and legs while in bed. Success! However, after a couple of days, he lost his left arm, and they had to go back in and do more scraping. Although he regained use of his arm, recovery would be long and painful. He spent a total of two weeks in the hospital. The real test would be getting him to stand up. I couldn't begin to imagine how painful and difficult that had to be. He told me it was excruciatingly painful. He felt like his head was going to crack right off his neck as if his neck simply could not hold the weight of his head. But every day they tried to get him to stand on his own. Then, he would need to take a couple of steps with the use of a walker. He was like a baby learning to take his first steps. That is how this process worked, step by step, and with a giant brace on his neck, he tried his best to do what he needed to do in order to learn how to walk again.

Chapter 2: The Big C

This was not the first time my caregiving skills were put to the test, although the circumstances were completely different. Over 15 years prior to this incident, my husband was diagnosed with Testicular Cancer, stage two. In order to make this diagnosis, they had to cut him open, leaving a good seven-inch swath spanning across his belly vertically. This was a surgery to determine what kind of cancer it was, which involved extracting lymph nodes from his spine. To access these lymph nodes, they had to remove all his internal organs, including his intestines. Once removed, the lymph nodes were examined on a hot slide to determine what kind of cancer it was. The determination was Seminoma, also known as Testicular Cancer, but fortunately, it had bypassed the testes and gone to the lymph nodes in his core, which is on top of his spinal cord.

Luckily, this type of cancer could be treated with an extremely lethal chemotherapy cocktail, which was all but guaranteed to eliminate the cancer, but at the cost of bringing him to the brink of death. This combination of chemicals included toxins designed to kill everything that replicated rapidly, including the cancer. However, the side effects were horrendous. According to the American Cancer Society, they included: hair loss, mouth sores, loss of appetite, nausea and vomiting, diarrhea, increased chance of infections (from having too few white blood cells), easy bruising or bleeding (from having too few blood platelets), and fatigue (extreme tiredness, often from having too few red blood cells) and believe me, he got all of them including some not mentioned on that list such as neuropathy and lung damage (Pulmonary Toxicity).

****

This all happened at a time in our lives when we made one of the biggest decisions we had ever made. To move from the house we built and lived in for 18 years (in San Diego County), where we raised our two children, to Sacramento, a place we knew nothing about. But my husband got *the* offer you couldn't refuse. Almost double pay in his industry and a chance to move up in the world, and with people he knew well and trusted.

This proved to be one of the greatest challenges of our lives! First, I had to quit the job I loved and find a new one in an unknown job market. Second, I had to sell our house and then find a new one in a city I knew nothing about. But, in order to sell the house, I had to fix everything the realtor said was wrong with it, which was somewhat of a slap in the face. I thought this house was already perfect, as it was our dream home. We built it ourselves, for goodness' sake!

Unbelievably, the 2,500 sq. ft. custom-built, split-level, ranch style home we built on two and one-half acres in rural San Diego did not sell right away. Admittedly, it was at the end of a five-mile winding road, which happened to be the longest cul-de-sac in rural San Diego County, but no matter, it was ours and it was beautiful!

While moving to Sacramento all sounded exciting at the time, there were many obstacles before we could actually make it happen. My husband had to go there ahead of us and get an apartment, mainly because he started his job before we could sell the house and find a new one in Sacramento. No problem except for the fact that I had a great job at the City of Chula Vista, my daughter was in her senior year in high school, my son was looking to move to Santa Barbara to start college, and I had no job prospects in Sacramento. It did not matter. This is what we decided we were going to do. I did not give this a second thought; I just dove right in without a life preserver and thought I would be okay. I just knew I could do this, we all thought we could do this…but the big C had something else in mind. Not two months into his new job, he called to tell me he had cancer.

However, before we knew any of this, the City Manager from my prior job gave me a stellar recommendation, and I was able to get a great position in Yolo County as the Economic Development Resource Coordinator for the entire county. This included West Sacramento, Woodland, Davis, and Winters. Not that economic development was extremely popular in a rural farmland county. Nevertheless, I felt as if fate had finally dealt me a winning hand.

This job enabled me to fly home on the weekends to attend to the kids and house, which I was still attempting to sell. But as happy and successful as I was in my new job, the situation at home soon became untenable, and being there for my kids in a crucial time in their lives had to take precedence. This situation had been building up for the last six months, and because the house still hadn't sold, I was in agony as to what to do. So, after talking to my husband and both my kids (17 and 19), the Director of the Public Works Department, and my boss, I made the decision to quit my job. Without a second thought, I packed my bags, kissed my understanding husband goodbye, and drove back to San Diego. I think I cried the entire way home.

My former boss, whom I loved dearly, was so dismayed over my impossible situation that she called me while I was driving back home from Sacramento to offer me a consulting job, which would enable me to have flexibility while doing everything that needed to be done. She literally saved me. With her help, I was able to start my own business as an independent contractor, fly from San Diego to Riverside, where my primary contract was, then back to Sacramento to take care of my husband.

This also enabled me to work on selling our home while allowing our daughter to graduate. Selling our home, it turned out, would not be easy. Our realtor informed us it was not a good time to sell as it was a buyer's market, and if we wanted to sell it quickly, there was a laundry list of work needed before we could put it on the market. So I had to suck it up, get my tool belt on, and get to work. However, I had to do it by myself, with no help from my husband, who, up until then, had always shown me how to do anything construction-oriented. We were partners and did everything together. But now I was on my own. Quite frankly, I wasn't even sure I knew how to use a drill motor. I certainly did not visualize myself with a sledgehammer and drill motor in hand, tearing out shelving and putting in drywall at this point in my life. After building the house, I thought my construction days were long gone…*"Nope!!"*

I remember one day in particular. I was in our garage, using a drill motor while lying on my back, upside down, trying to install a simple shelf. But first, I had to figure out which switch was reverse and which one was forward on that fangled contraption, while trying to avoid getting sawdust in my eyes in the process. I quickly learned just how much strength was needed to push hard enough to get the screw in without stripping it, within a very confined space. Kind of like being in a coffin with a drill, trying desperately to get the screws out before losing air. As if that wasn't bad enough, a rather large black widow spider made its way down on an invisible web to check out what the heck I was doing, disturbing her territory. So, I did what any fearless Woman of the Universe would do in that situation, stifled a scream, turned off my very noisy drill motor, and slowly scooted away on my back, then got up, and proceeded to do the hebee-gebee dance. You know the one—you flail around wildly as if being attacked by killer bees.

Feeling utterly defeated, I brushed myself off, sat down on the cold garage floor, and proceeded to cry for a good half hour. I certainly did not feel like I was properly representing my formidable and indomitable female sisterhood in the way they should be represented. I failed because it was too hard. *"I shouldn't be doing this in the first place. I hate black widows, and I ruined both my shirt and my pants!"* Not that I had any attachment to them, but it was a matter of principle.

After all that hard work, the house *still* did not sell right away. In fact, it would take another six months. But it gave us time for my daughter to graduate with all her friends and classmates. It also gave my son time to move to Santa Barbara, where he would live with his cousin and attend college while working at three part-time jobs. It gave me time to look for a new home in Sacramento, complete my contract, all while caring for my husband. In my mind, this was all manageable, looking for a house and a job and taking care of my husband in Sacramento during the week and then going home to San Diego to take care of the kids on the weekends. *"I had this!"*

While all this was going on, my husband was going through chemotherapy while still working, that is, until it became impossible for him to do so. The chemotherapy was so harsh it ravaged his skin, muscles, and, sadly, he lost every hair on his body (including his eyebrows). I remember flying back to Sacramento, picking him up at the treatment center, and then seeing him collapse on the couch. There were times I literally had to bend over close to his nose and mouth just to see if he was still breathing. He looked so pale that he could have been dead for all intents and purposes. The treatment protocol lived up to its reputation and brought my husband to the brink of death.

Although I never used the word caregiving, that is exactly what I was doing. Caregiver wasn't a term widely used or known at the time. My job description as his wife included cooking meals, doing laundry, cleaning the apartment, running errands, administering medication, checking his vitals, making sure he was comfortable, basically keeping him alive, and driving him back and forth from treatment to our little temporary apartment in Sacramento. I tried to be there for him every step of the way, while doing my consulting job, selling the house, finding a new one, helping the kids apply to college, and all while trying to stay sane.

I don't know how we made it, but we did. My husband survived chemotherapy, the cancer was in remission, but left him with Neuropathy and an awful lung disorder (Pulmonary Toxicity).

Fortunately, the lung disorder would diminish somewhat, but the Neuropathy never went away. However, to us, it was a small price to pay for saving his life. He did four rounds of the harshest chemotherapy treatment there was, and lived to tell his story, which is exactly what he did.

Finally, we sold our home and settled in a beautiful new home in Elk Grove. The two-story home was 2,700 sq ft. with four bedrooms, three baths, an open concept great room, living room, and dining room, and a chef's kitchen with lots of counter and cabinet space. The backyard was paradise with a gorgeous lagoon-style pool and rock waterfall, a spa jacuzzi, all in a setting resembling Hawaii. It was gorgeous and made leaving San Diego a little more tolerable.

Conveniently, my daughter was accepted to UC Davis and would live in a dorm with her new college buddies. My son went to Santa Barbara as planned, to attend junior college, while working three jobs *(What?!!)*. My husband continued to work for the same company, and I continued consulting until I completed my contract.

Just about this time, my husband heard about a National writing competition that was being sponsored by the very pharmaceutical company (Amgen) that made the chemotherapy treatment he was on. My husband, an already accomplished writer, didn't hesitate and began writing the 500-word-or-less essay about his Cancer Coach, which was me. The winner would be flown to New York City for four days and five nights, and attend the men's college Basketball Playoff games at Madison Square Garden and sit in the same seats as ESPN!. Oh, and did I mention all expenses paid?!

Well, he wrote a beautiful story that nearly broke my heart to read. He entered it into the drawing, and as time went by, we both forgot all about it. Besides, we both knew the chances of him winning were slim to none. So when we received a letter from Amgen, we both nearly passed out. We were one of two winners in the National writing contest. We had won the grand prize and were going to New York City, bay-bee!

Now, I always knew my husband was a good writer, but this was the icing on the cake of good fortune! This was his winning story:

"Honey," I said into my cell phone, "the doctors think I have cancer." Hundreds of miles away, my wife Shelly put her emotions on hold, asking pragmatic questions. "I don't know yet," was my canned response, "but I will know more soon." After I hung up, she cried alone on the side of the freeway, and I went back to work at my new job, in a new city. I commuted twice a week on planes, as we tried to sell our house, move, and become a one-city family again.

In 26 years together, we had built our own home, raised two children, and were now establishing a new home in another city to improve our lot. Then Life grabbed the steering wheel and veered us in a new direction. It started with the doctor's suspicions, morphed into a major surgery biopsy, and concluded with four rounds of chemotherapy. For nine months, The Big C was in charge of our lives. But I had a secret weapon on the battlefield of chemo called positive attitude, and an abundant source of it nearby, named Shelly. She taught me that in surviving cancer, what goes on between the ears has more to say about Quality of Life than what happens from the neck down.

She never let the harsh reality creep in too far, injecting color into a world that chemo had reduced to black and white. She would check my shallow breathing as I slept, stuffing her fear that it might stop arbitrarily. I drifted from the conscious world to the unconscious with alarming regularity, as life's simplest tasks overwhelmed me with fatigue. Lethargy settled like a wet blanket, and I felt like an insect trapped in gooey, unrelenting amber. Nothing was easy to do anymore.

With Shelly's help, I garnered the will to extract myself. We cherished our time together as never before. We laughed as I pulled my hair out in clumps, we joked about the "chemo-diet to a slimmer, trimmer, you," and I enjoyed the freedom of not having to shave my face every morning for many months. And we cried, too, about the harshness of this disease, about the flagging skin that hung on my skinny body and the perverseness of having a fat face at the same time; of the constant nausea, that allowed only the briefest, unpleasant moments of respite; of the "Godzilla hiccups" that would rack my body in the middle of the night, waking Shelly in a panic; of chemo's nerve damage to my feet, robbing me of all feeling below my ankles permanently.

Shelly gave me back the hope that chemo tried to wash away, even though she had the more difficult task. I had an enemy to fight directly, while she had to wait, watching me deteriorate, and nurture me from the periphery. Eventually, the chemo sent the cancer into remission (maybe forever), and Shelly loved me back from the cliff edge, returning color to my world.

Although my first experience as a Caregiver may have been tough, it did not prepare me for what caregiving really entailed. However, when the time came, I gave it my all, not knowing that everything I did would not help him recover…he would never recover, but I didn't know that. So I went along blindly doing what I was supposed to do in hopes that one day he would walk again.

Part II:
Crisis &
Transition

Chapter 3: From Hospital Halls To Home

The day finally came when he was released from the hospital and admitted to a convalescent hospital for rehabilitation and physical therapy. Now, I had never seen a convalescent facility before, so I didn't know what to expect. From the moment I walked in, I was hit with a smell I can only describe as a mix of rotting sickness and dirty sheets. I felt nauseated. The walls, furniture and carpeting resembled a 70's motif with drab and faded colors such as avocado green, orange, pink and yellow. It looked as if they had raided a garage sale and got the oldest, most worn-out, faded furniture they could find, dusted it off, and for a modest price, called it good.

Patients with tubes and IVs on wheels shuffled by slowly, not looking up but focused on the floor ahead of them. I made my way to the front desk, which looked remarkably like the nurses' station at the ER. No one paid any attention to me until I flagged someone down, who made it very clear I was interrupting something more important, but managed to be somewhat civil.

Once I indicated I wanted the room number of my husband, who had just been admitted, his demeanor changed, and the rehearsed polite patient representative whisked me away from the front desk and down a long hall. Most of the doors were open, allowing passersby to hear the wailing, yelling, and crying, and to get a full view of those obviously not moving anytime soon. I stifled a sob and turned away, looking straight ahead, hoping the rooms I just saw had no relation to the room my husband would be in.

We stopped in front of a door like any other and walked in. A curtain divided the room with two patients. The first patient was incoherent. He lay there in a state of malaise, mumbling conversations to no one. We quickly moved to the next bed only to find it empty. Alarmed, I looked at the orderly, and he looked as confused as I was. He told me to wait there, and he would find out where he was. When he left, I took the opportunity to check out the room. The first thing I noticed was an old, stained floral bedspread that looked like it had been washed too many times. There was a window, but it only had a view of the parking lot. The curtains were orange tweed and looked equally old and dingy, stained with a dusty brown strip at the bottom where it rested on the dirty windowsill.

I peered cautiously into the shared bathroom and immediately regretted it. There was urine in the stained toilet, surrounded by old, yellowed linoleum that curled up on the edges. The floor around the sink and toilet was stained, and the toilet paper hung down to the floor, tinged on the edges with a color I care not to mention. There was an empty urinal in the sink that had obviously not been cleaned out. But the smell was the clincher… I quickly exited the tiny room and just as

I came through the door, my husband, accompanied by an attendant, scuffled in with his walker, looking at his feet, not even noticing I was there.

The look on my husband's face told me everything. He was in pain, but there was also a look that can only be described as disillusionment. However, the moment he saw me, his face lit up, and he smiled, probably for the first time in a long time. I immediately teared up and fought the urge to bawl my eyes out. But I simply helped him get into his small single bed, which was not easy. He was exhausted from a very short walk down the hall with a walker and the assistance of an aide. He had a belt around him with a leash just in case he fell. We had to take off the apparatus before lowering him slowly onto the bed, being ever so careful to brace his neck as we lowered it onto the pillow. The process was horrendously painful, and I could see tears welling up in his eyes. I had to turn away and let the orderly do his job, while I politely stepped out of his way, trying not to let him see the horrified look on my face.

Pretending to look at the view out the window, I let the aide finish tucking him in until he walked out. When I turned to look at him, his strained face had found a way to look cheerful and happy to see me. And as happy as I was to see him, I had to hide my troubles and put on a good face. The last few days had been stressful, but he had no idea what I had been dealing with. I was in the process of moving us from living in an RV to an apartment, a requirement for his release, which meant his stay at this horrid facility could be extended. But I had to put my fears and problems on hold as I hadn't seen him for a couple of days, and apparently, a lot happened in that short span of time.

He recited a litany of complaints about the type of care he was receiving. The most heinous of these complaints made my skin crawl. He had a very loose bowel movement in the middle of the night and rang for help, and he sat in his own excrement for over three hours before someone finally came in to change him. Livid and succumbing to my already stressed-out demeanor, I marched out to the front desk and demanded to talk to the head nurse or supervising physician immediately. My voice level commanded the attention of everyone at the front desk, and I was directed to the facility manager in short order. Keenly aware of onlookers and potential customers, he quickly guided me to a private office. By that time, my blood was boiling, and I unleashed with a fury that can only be described as "The Psycho Bitch from Hell." Starting with the worst… midnight bowel movement, I rattled off several things I found completely unacceptable. Of course, he apologized profusely and told me he would personally look into the situation. Temporary placation complete, I walked out feeling somewhat vindicated.

An illusion… that is what it was… I had no real victory. I would not be victorious until he was released. The reality was that healthcare workers there were underpaid and overworked... a common theme in this industry. I remember him telling me he had chicken nuggets that tasted like cardboard, on stale waffles with syrup for breakfast. That is just wrong… on so many levels! I had to get him out of there, but that would prove to be a very difficult process. These facilities thrived on insurance payments from Medicare and Medicaid, which made it that much more difficult to get him out of there. They would be the ones making that determination. However, I had the secret weapon… my husband. Little did they know, he had the determination of a gold medal Olympian… and he was going for the gold. He would beat the odds and show them that they couldn't keep him down for long. Besides… he hated the place. He wanted out in the worst way. A plan was set in motion. Game on!

In reality, I never knew when I could visit him, because I had two priorities. First of all, he couldn't come home unless I had a legitimate home for him to go to. A motor home did not qualify. So I was scrambling to find something on very short notice. This is where the family came to my aid. My sister-in-law, a big honcho in a property management company with many properties at her disposal, found a beautiful condo in Mission Valley, which she knew I could afford, on the first floor, and no stairs… perfect! Of course, it was temporary housing, but we could have it for three months, which gave me more time to find something permanent.

The second priority was to visit him as often as possible and bring his favorite food and snacks. He was the envy of all who knew him… and believe me… he made friends wherever he went. In little or no time, he befriended a contingent of people who would come to visit him…one in particular who called himself Mexican Art. He was the self-appointed Mayor of the place, and no one disputed or challenged his authority. He welcomed any and all who came in… including me, and I got special priority because he knew who I was, and when I arrived in heels and in a Jeep Wrangler, my status immediately went up. Ba-zing! So, I was personally escorted to my husband's room, and he often joined in the wonderful goodies I brought.

On many occasions, I would show up and he would not be in his room, which usually meant he was in physical therapy. He never saw me come in because he was in deep concentration on whatever exercise they were doing. The strain on his face told me this was more difficult than either of us thought. Clearly, this was going to take every bit of time and energy he had at his disposal, which was all the time in the world. After watching him clandestinely, I would break out a round of applause so he would know I was there supporting him. He couldn't turn around, so his physical therapist told him I was there cheering him on. Almost immediately, he started showing off, doing things he probably shouldn't be doing, but he was desperate to show me his progress, which would get him that much closer to leaving that god forsaken place. But the reality was, his progress would be slow and painful, and when he was finally able to get back to bed, he all but collapsed. However, to his credit, he had a remarkably great attitude, which, given his situation, would be extremely difficult for anyone to do. Myself included. Although I felt terrified inside, I was in awe of his ability to put on a good face.

When the release date approached, we were bombarded with information, procedures for medication administration, care instructions, physical therapy, follow-up appointments and, of course, release papers that needed to be signed before he could officially leave. The head nurse asked very matter-of-factly, "Are you going to be his caregiver?" That was the first time anyone had ever asked me that, and I had no idea what saying "yes" actually meant. The instructions given to me could have fit in a four-inch binder; it was arduous, to say the least. But she handed it to me with very little care as to whether or not I knew what to do. "Everything you need to know is in that binder. His primary care doctor will be his contact now." She handed me the paperwork, a bag of his personal belongings, and I waited by the Jeep, my only vehicle, as he was wheeled out to me. Then it hit me…I had nothing. No cane, no walker, no wheelchair… nothing. Yet, it took two men to get him into the Jeep. "What was I thinking? How was I going to get him out of the Jeep?" I panicked… "Wait," I cried. "I don't have any help or equipment!" They gave me a walker that I needed to return once I had procured one of my own.

It's shocking to think about things you'd never even consider when driving with a spinal cord injury patient. That 15-minute ride to our new place was exhausting. He was not used to driving in a car, and it seemed to him as if we were speeding, although I was actually going painfully slow, conscious of every little bump or stop we made. He later admitted that he was petrified riding in the car with me. He explained that he felt extremely vulnerable and exposed. It had been over a month since he'd been in a car, so every little bump, turn and stop was painful. He freaked out, and that made driving extremely difficult and stressful. Talk about the back seat driver, he was the paranoid schizophrenic patient with a neck injury from hell! And let's not talk about speed bumps, although there were quite a few by the hospital and by the foo-foo condo complex we now lived in. By the time we got to the condo, I was a wreck! Thankfully, my son was there to help and, assessing the situation, quickly took over and managed to get him to the front door and over to the couch, where he collapsed.

It wasn't until much later that he actually saw his new surroundings. I had managed to get a totally furnished condo in Mission Valley—a gated community—with all the comforts of home. Everything we needed was there, and the rest was in storage, a place where remnants of our past lives were stored. He looked around and smiled. He approved of the place, and I was so happy. I had worked hard to make it comfortable for him. It was sparse, but it was home for now, and we were lucky to have it. We would only get it for three months, until we could find a more permanent place to live.

Fortunately, my husband could still walk (with a walker), go to the bathroom by himself and feed himself. He still had some fine motor skills, which, I've come to realize, we all take for granted, such as picking up anything heavy or light; exerting pressure to push a button, or switch; putting on his glasses, turning a handle or typing on a keyboard. Peripheral Neuropathy took some of the feeling from his hands and feet, but after surgery, these symptoms became severely diminished. Over the next eight years, it would continue to worsen. This is where the real caregiving began. Although I had no idea what that would mean or entail.

As time went on, the stark reality of being a caregiver hit me smack in the face. I don't know…perhaps I thought he'd come home and start living life like he used to… ummmm… no! The very effort of getting up and walking to the couch with a walker was exhausting. He slept most of the day. Even talking was exhaustive. I spent most of my time keeping him comfortable and doing research to find a wheelchair, walker, diapers, pads, gauze, antiseptic… "Ahhhhhhh! What was I thinking?" I was so unprepared for someone who had just had major surgery on his neck, with a scar that went from the base of his neck to the middle of his back. Let's not talk about medications, my goodness! Starting with Morphine, there were anti-inflammatories, antibiotics, muscle relaxants, steroids, ointments and medication I had to look up to know what it was. Of course, the book they gave me had all the instructions and medications I needed to know, but just looking at it was overwhelming and in some cases required a magnifying glass.

This was certainly a challenging time, but not the only one. We were blessed with multiple challenges in our lifetime, which should make us super humans by now…right? Or at least SuperGirl, as my husband could never maneuver putting on a Superman suit in a phone booth if his life depended on it. So, that was it…the dye was cast…I would be his SuperGirl, wife, nurse, cook, housekeeper, shopper, financial manager, and of course, SUPER CAREGIVER!!!

Chapter 4: Caring for Two

When I look back at this time, I realize I was not just a caregiver for my husband, but for my mom as well, and the timing couldn't have been worse. I had just moved all our belongings from our motor home to our new place in Mission Valley. The rest would have to go into storage. As exhausted as I was after packing and unpacking, my responsibilities did not end there.

My parents still relied on me for many things, one of them being entertaining out-of-town guests. My mom had asked me to stop by for a brief visit, which we both knew was not the case. She had not been feeling well and needed me to help her prepare a meal and get the guest room ready. She was well aware of what I was going through, but no matter, her needs came first. I complied because I had not seen our cousins for almost 20 years, and I was very excited to see them.

Now, my mom prided herself on being a great hostess and would typically be ecstatic about seeing anyone from Michigan (her childhood home), but this time she was totally unprepared and certainly not her enthusiastic self. My dad noticed too and told her to go lie down." "Shelly and I can handle it," he said, somewhat convincingly. So I stepped in as hostess and did my best to keep them entertained, even though we were all noticeably concerned.

I occasionally went upstairs to check on her, and she was feverish, nauseated, and weak. She spent the rest of that day and the next in bed, and both my dad and I knew something was very wrong. But when she became incoherent, we decided to take her to the Emergency Room. I quickly arranged for my son to look after my husband so I could accompany my dad to the ER.

My dad and I waited for what seemed like hours until they finally told us they would be admitting her to the hospital with pneumonia, and I felt somewhat relieved. She would be cared for, and I could go home and take care of my husband. But just as I got my husband comfortable, which was an ordeal with that brace on his neck, the phone rang.

It was my mom, and I could tell she had been crying. In her weak and shaky voice, she told me she had cancer. Stage 4 colon cancer. I don't remember much because I think I was in a state of shock. How could this be? Why was this happening? She had been fine—we had gone out to lunch together just a week prior to bringing my husband home. My world was collapsing, and all I could think about was how I was going to be there for my mom while taking care of my husband.

I had so many questions, and I knew straight away I had to be her advocate and help my dad, who, naturally, was a wreck. I had experience in this situation, and no one else in the family was able to do this, so it fell on me. When talking with the oncologist, I was familiar with the lingo and able to ask the right questions. Of course, a regimen of chemo treatments was recommended that would have horrific side effects with no guarantee of remission.

Both my parents decided to go for it with an unrealistic outlook on her recovery. However, I looked at her test results and CT scan and knew it had metastasized to her liver. Recovery at this stage was less than 20 percent. Even with treatment, it would only extend her life by months…maybe. But her quality of life would suffer, and that was something neither one of them wanted to hear.

With encouragement from the oncologist, they were going down a long and painful road. They only heard what they wanted to hear, and common sense was out of the question. I tried to convince my dad to look into palliative care, but he looked at me like I had just recommended her death sentence. With all the knowledge and time I spent trying to help them come to the right decision for Mom, they completely ignored my advice and started chemo treatments. The doctor was no help either. After all, they aren't trained to help people die, only how to keep them living, no matter the cost.

After five months of miserable treatments, my mom had lost over 30 lbs. (pounds she did not have to lose) and could not, or would not, eat anything substantial. She slept most of the time and had very little energy when she wasn't napping. The next round of CT scans showed little to no improvement, but they still didn't want to face the alternative. Feeling utterly defeated and frustrated, I returned home and back to caring for my husband full-time.

By this time, I had moved us to a 500 sq. ft. apartment located conveniently near the hospital and my husband's neurologist. Our son moved in with us and slept on the couch. He had just gone through a painful divorce, had been diagnosed with bipolar disorder, and had tried to commit suicide. We drove to Santa Barbara to rescue him. So, to get the record straight, I was caring for my husband, my son, and my mom.

My daughter had been accepted to UC Davis and was deep into her educational journey, living in dorms and pursuing two bachelor's degrees. Understandably, she could not break away. Just when I thought things 'couldn't get any worse, my mom slipped and fell while hosing off the patio in her high heels and broke her hip. This was the beginning of the end.

Her stint in the hospital was brief, and when they could no longer do anything for her, she was quickly transferred to a skilled nursing facility. Not much better than the one my husband had been in, she also shared a room with another patient, and my dad and I visited almost every day. She faded in and out of consciousness but said nothing that gave us any comfort. There were no words of regret, no expressions of love, no apologies.

In fact, the last words my mother uttered to me were instructions to get the skirt she had on when she got there, before the EMTs arrived. She didn't want to be seen in the hospital gown she was wearing. "REALLY???!!!"

Her cancer progressed because they could no longer administer her chemotherapy treatments in that facility, and it became necessary for her to be on morphine to manage the pain. Again, playing the bad guy, I suggested hospice care and was shot down. She had to suffer some more, I guess. But when the time came that she could no longer stand up to walk (a requirement of being in that facility), I had a meeting with the head nurse, and we knew it was time to get hospice involved.

By this time, my dad was worthless. He finally gave in to my wishes, and I quickly got her transferred home and enlisted hospice to aid in her comfort.

It was as if everyone in my family had blinders on, and my mom suffered because of it. She passed the next day at the home she loved, with family surrounding her. Actually, not all of that was true, as my family was still in denial. Although I tried to tell everyone to get there quickly because I knew she was fading, most weren't there. And those who were, were in the kitchen talking with the hospice nurses about comfort care.

Meanwhile, I was with her in the den, holding her ice-cold hand and singing the same nursery songs she sang to me when I was little. I whispered in her ear that she was a good mother and that everyone loved her. I told her all the people she had lost were waiting for her to come home. I watched her take her last breath and burst into tears, releasing all the months of pain, anguish, and stress at once.

I Am a Caregiver

Everyone rushed into the den in disbelief. The hospice nurses checked her vitals and confirmed her passing. The level of caregiving I administered to my mom was more psychological than physical. Although I did visit her every day at the nursing home, ran errands for her, made special meals for her, and went to treatments and doctor appointments with her (since my dad was all but deaf and couldn't hear what the doctor was saying), I also sat by her in her bedroom and watched daytime soaps with her. I had conference calls with her doctor to get her the right meds for all her side effects. I cleaned her house for her, and at the end, I was there when she died.

All this while caring for a husband who was recovering from a spinal cord injury and subsequent corrective surgery, and helping my son rebuild his life and self-confidence with all the love and support we could give him.

The next month was given to closing the chapter on my mom's life as I planned her Celebration of Life gathering. The time had come to say the final goodbye, and we did so with a slideshow of pictures of her at every age and stage of her glamorous life, catered food, music (her favorite), friends, and family—all at the house she loved and lived in for almost 50 years. She would have liked her send-off, and I hoped she would have been there as we all honored her life and said our goodbyes.

"Goodbye, Mom."

Once I turned my attention back to the little apartment I found close to the hospital where my husband had his surgery, I desperately tried to make that tiny space feel homey. I decorated it in aqua blue, with one wall depicting a beach scene using fishnet and seashells. The effect was meant to create a sense of calm and relaxation.

As much as I tried to make it comfortable for him, those first few months were miserable. There were countless sleepless nights, filled with stomach-wrenching cramps and endless episodes of loose stool. I was certain I couldn't change one more poopy diaper, and on many occasions, I seriously thought about leaving him behind and running off to Bora Bora.

Unbelievably, we did get through it, but many other challenges still lay ahead. Difficult as it was for him to navigate his wheelchair in that tiny apartment, somehow, through sheer determination, he found his ground and was able to make his way around with little or no help. But his internal digestive problems never really went away, and how could they? The previous testicular cancer surgery he underwent involved removing all his intestines and somehow placing all 22 feet of small intestine and six feet of large intestine back inside him exactly as they had been before. I still don't know how that was even possible, but they did it, and he had never been the same since.

One particular night I'll never forget. It was so bad…I had used every towel, sheet, and scrap of clothing I could find to soak up the deluge of fecal matter that all but ruined the mattress we slept on. I never knew a person could have so much inside them. I remember standing in the laundry room two doors down from our apartment, sobbing as I scrubbed endless poop-covered, stinking towels, sheets, and clothing in the sink before putting them in the washer, praying no one would walk in. It was 1:00 in the morning, so I thought my chances were good, but sure enough, someone came in and witnessed the horrible debacle.

I can't imagine how I must have looked, perhaps like a woman who had just cleaned out every sewer pipe in San Diego County with dead puppy carcasses. I was ruined and wasn't sure if I could ever recover. But I did. Although I seriously considered divorce and wondered why I had ever married this man in the first place.

The next day, when all was settled, I reconsidered my position and, looking at my poor husband who had just been through hell, decided I'd give him another chance. There were many days and nights like that, but eventually his stomach settled, we got a diet plan in place, and those incidents happened less and less.

In order to get this place, and to truly readjust our mode of living and transportation, we had to sell the motorhome (our road gypsy home for three years) and my Jeep Wrangler. Turns out it was not built for anyone with a neck injury. First of all, it was too difficult to get into, and secondly, the wheelchair would not fit in it. I was devastated. That Jeep Wrangler and I had some hair-raising and fantastically fun times together (most of which my husband didn't know about). I could go anywhere in that Jeep, which made going rockhounding (my passion) so much easier and more accessible.

I remember one of our first trips to Opal Mountain near Red Rock Canyon in Arizona. While this site was known for its Common Opal deposits, what many did not know, myself included, was that it also had a rich deposit of white, lavender, and pink agate. But to get to it, you had to take a very narrow and rocky dirt road to the top plateau. And when I say rocky, I mean boulder-rocky…very dicey! Once at the top, though, the view was spectacular, but what I was standing on was even more so. A carpet of lavender, pink, and white agate spread before me and with pick and shovel in hand, I gathered some beautiful specimens. Only a few, though—I always made sure there was plenty left for the next rockhounder. The trip was dangerous, but it was worth it, and we had my little beetle-wing green Jeep Wrangler (Sahara) to thank for it. We had some good times, but it was time to say goodbye. *"Adios, my friend!"*

****

Now, admittedly, our apartment was small, but when my son came to live with us, that 500 sq. ft. space became claustrophobic in a very short period of time. It became obvious rather quickly that we had to move into something a little bigger, with a room for our son should he decide to stay with us. His tumultuous journey was spent in large part with us, no matter where we were or under what conditions…we were family, and we were going to do everything we could to help him recover. Help us all recover.

Yes, we did find another two-bedroom, two-bath apartment, but it was in El Cajon, a suburb of San Diego, which I was not particularly fond of, but it fit our needs and budget at the time. We had a view of the pool and front door access to the gym, so one would think that sounded pretty good"… *NO*"*!* The late-night beer parties and prostitutes who used the pool restrooms as a temporary meeting place with their Johns made living there intolerable.

We made it one year and quickly decided to throw in the towel and go back to Sacramento to be close to our daughter. Our son came with us and, within one week of looking, we found a beautiful condo surrounded by redwoods, in a gated community with all the amenities. Housing was so much cheaper in Sacramento, and moving from El Cajon to South Natomas seemed like going from rags to riches. It really was perfect, but no sooner had we settled there than we found ourselves in a position to buy a home again, much closer to Davis and the grandkids, and that's exactly what we did.

Part III:

Love and

Perspective

Chapter 5: My Dad

While my mom was still with us, my dad had a series of health issues resulting in endless trips to his doctor and specialists to figure out what was going on. My dad was hard of hearing, and even with hearing aids, he struggled to hear well enough to understand or even participate in a conversation. Most of the time, he would shake his head up and down in acknowledgement, but really had no idea what he was acknowledging. I wound up going on many of these appointments with him as an interpreter, and because my mom could not and would not deal with anything having to do with caregiving. She told me point-blank, "I am not a caregiver," and that was that. As no one else stepped up to the plate, the burden fell on me, and because I was not working, I had the time. My brother worked full-time, and my sister lived an hour away. It simply made sense that I take over.

My dad had a myriad of mysterious symptoms, making a diagnosis very difficult. But in watching my dad, I knew something serious was going on. I implored the doctors to run more tests. After doing extensive online research on my own, I made several suggestions as to what might be going on. The pain in his back caused him the most distress, and the doctors prescribed painkillers, physical therapy, and steroid injections to no avail. Finally, after months of going around in circles and reading medical studies online, I suggested that he might have an infection. I insisted on blood work that would specifically look for that.

The doctor was just as frustrated as I was and was willing to try just about anything to make it go away. Sure enough, the blood work came back indicating he had a staph infection in his blood, which stemmed from wires left in his chest from a pacemaker that was removed. The wires were left there because they were too close to his heart, and there was a fear that he could bleed out on the operating table if they tried to remove them. He had been on blood thinners for years because of Atrial Fibrillation. This was just one of many things my dad suffered through, including Thyroid Cancer when he was in his twenties, which was extremely difficult to treat back then. He survived the surgery only to find out his vocal cords were damaged, which made his voice very deep and scratchy.

After the diagnosis was confirmed, the doctors opted for suppressive antibiotic therapy, which is a non-curative strategy that involves the long-term administration of antibiotics. It is a palliative approach, often considered when other conventional management is unfeasible or suboptimal.[5] In this case, surgery was not an option. Within weeks of this intravenous treatment, all his symptoms, including back pain, went away. Turns out I was getting rather good at

---

[5] Infectious Diseases Now, Volume 54, Issue 3, April, 2024

asking the right questions when it came to health and symptom diagnostics.

Years passed, and my dad maintained what I would call good health, considering he was in his eighties. But what none of us knew was that my dad had a ticking time bomb inside him. Although he managed to stay active, even after my mom died, he got tired easily, and he started losing a lot of weight—two signs that signaled a red flag to me. No matter…ever the ladies' man, he traveled and met women his age and younger wherever he went.

Through a chance introduction, my dad met the woman he would eventually fall in love with, and there were a few good years where they traveled and spent most of their time together. But just as things started getting serious, I noticed his stomach protruded even though he was very thin, and his veins were visible all over his torso. I had encouraged my dad to see a doctor, but he procrastinated. He had his fill of doctors after having spent hours at the ear, nose, and eye doctor for a variety of issues stemming from hearing loss, severe allergies, and glaucoma.

My dad was in the midst of planning a trip to China and purchasing a home with his new lady friend when he began to succumb to the monster growing inside him. No one in the family had any clue that he had been suffering because he never slowed down. We had all been concerned about him. He did not look good and always complained about how tired he was whenever I visited. This time, I insisted he go to the doctor, and they did a series of tests and lab work. I remember him calling me to tell me he got his test results back. Always the comedian, he told me he wasn't a good test taker, as if he were back in school. I, of course, asked him to send the report to me, and at 10:00 pm, I printed out the report and crawled into bed to read the results. I had barely started reading the first page when I felt my face flush, and my stomach knot up.

The report stated that he had tumors in his kidneys, liver, stomach, and pancreas. 'My god,' I thought. 'He has pancreatic cancer! Bad test taking?'

He must have known what the report indicated, and surely the doctor told him what was going on. But he joked about it, and within a few days after getting the report, he collapsed and was rushed to the hospital with pneumonia in both lungs. I booked the first flight out to San Diego and arrived just in time to say goodbye. He told my brother, while in the hospital, that he didn't want any more treatment and just wanted to go home. By the time I got there, he was incoherent, his breathing was rattly, and his skin was cold and clammy. With family and hospice nurses around him, he passed within hours after my arrival.

My dad had been suffering from Stage four Pancreatic Cancer, and how he managed to live day to day as if nothing was wrong will always be a mystery. Ironically, his last words to me were a deception... he knew what he had, but none of us knew until it was too late. I had to read the report rather than hear it from my dad. So very sad… I did not get to say the things I would have liked him to know. But whether he heard me or not… I told him I loved him and that he was a good dad.

"Goodbye, Dad."

Chapter 6: Dandelion

It's widely known that animals have a special healing effect on us. Just the motion of petting or caressing an animal can calm us and alleviate stress. Animals have been used to help the elderly and chronically ill, and studies have shown a positive healing connection between animals and people with mental illness. Animals have the ability to form a bond with us that we find hard to duplicate. They give us unconditional love.

Rarely has there ever been a time when there weren't animals in my life. Pictures of when I was very little show me with a precious little dog named Snopsy-Baby… all white with a black eye. As far back as I can remember, there were either dogs or cats or both in our lives. They were a constant source of joy and entertainment, especially when my kids were growing up.

Unfortunately, they were also a source of profound pain when they were gravely ill or passed away unexpectedly. For all the love they gave us, there was an equal amount of pain and sadness when they left us. This is the case with the last animal I had. A cat I named Dandelion.

She came to us at the apartment in Mission Valley, during the time when my mom was dying and my husband had just had major spinal cord surgery. I wasn't the one who spotted her. My husband did, and he wasn't even a cat person. But she had found our sliding glass door, looking, no doubt, for food and shelter. I really don't know how old she was when she found us because she was so emaciated, it was hard to tell. From what I could tell at the time, she had long gray and orangish hair and beautiful green eyes. I later learned she was a Maine Coon.

Someone had deserted her and was cruel to her. She did not trust anyone… even me… a cat lover. I swear, there were times when stray cats would just come to me out of nowhere and ignore everyone else. My husband called me the pied piper of kitties. But this kitty was wary and would run every time I came outside the sliding glass door. So I would come out and place chicken in a dish on the concrete outside the slider. Eventually, she would hop up on the stucco wall enclosing our small patio and, with lightning speed, snatch up the chicken and run into the bushes. She'd drop it in the dirt and then eat it ravenously.

Why she sought out our patio is beyond me. There were many first-floor apartments with the same set-up. She chose ours. I often reflect back on that time and wonder if it was simply meant to be. She needed me, and I needed her. But getting her to trust me would not be easy. I worked at it for a few days…placing the chicken closer and closer to the chair where I sat on our patio. Until finally, she took the meat from my hand and ran back to the safety of the bushes. That was progress, so I got bolder and put the meat in a dish on my lap. With a soothing voice, I coaxed her to me, reassuring her that everything would be okay. She jumped up on my lap and I petted her for the first time using soothing words and whispers. She started to purr. She was mine!

From that point on, we were inseparable. I think she longed to be inside like she had been before she was abandoned. So when I opened the door to our living room…she did not hesitate and ran in as if she had just come home. Once inside, she never wanted to go outside ever again. It was a jungle out there, and she had seen her share of close calls and scary encounters. She was an inside kitty, and that is how it would stay. The joy and adulation of finally finding someone to love her was overwhelming. She slept between my husband and me (something my husband would never allow before), and would roll on her back exposing her belly for a rub, which left her extremely vulnerable. But she trusted us and allowed us to lavish her with tummy rubs and caresses. We loved her and she loved us. However, she couldn't have come to us at a more tumultuous time in our lives.

First things first, I took her to the veterinarian for her shots and anything else she might need. I suspected she had ear mites as she lived outside in god knows what kind of conditions, and she shook her head quite a bit, indicating an ear problem. One of her little ears flattened out, which told me it was bothering her. I also had her de-flead and eventually had her spayed. The vet cleaned out her ears and gave me drops. She hated them. Once she gained some weight and regained her healthy luster, she was absolutely beautiful.

She eventually shied away from my husband and bonded with me as her momma. She slept only with me, usually at my feet or head, which meant I could not move. But I gladly gave up that luxury for her. She shunned all others—mostly men—like my son, especially if he wore black pants. I had the feeling she had been abused by a man with black pants, who may have hit her with a broom. She hated brooms. She would run and hide under the bed the minute anyone touched the broom. We all puzzled over her past, trying to fit the pieces together, but the truth was, we would never know what misery she lived through. She was with me now, and I promised I would never abandon her.

Unfortunately, she would have to endure four moves in four years; the worst would be from San Diego to Sacramento. Did I mention she hated riding in cars? I had to get a kitty carrying case, and it seemed she knew what that was, too. The minute I got it out, she ran under the bed. So we had our little struggles, but mom always won, one way or the other.

Nonetheless, moving was always traumatic for her. She would hide for a couple of days until she felt it was okay to come out. But once she did, she owned the place. Then there were times I had to leave for days at a time, mostly to care for my dad in San Diego. But upon return, Dandelion would ignore me for a while, just to let me know she did not approve of my leaving without her. But it never lasted long, and once forgiven, I was her best bud again.

Dandelion

We finally settled into our new home in Woodland, California, which was ten minutes from Davis, where my daughter and grandkids lived. At that time, my son was still with us, and he and Dandelion had become good buds. He had endured four moves as well. She put up with his rough-and-tumble style of belly rubs and kitty pets and never once bit, scratched, or growled at all. She was the only kitty I ever had that didn't do that. Typically, I would have scratches on my hands and arms from rough kitty play, but not with her. She was gentle and very reserved, and when she didn't like something, she would gently put her paw on you and push just enough to let you know that was all she was going to put up with.

The one thing that never failed to amaze me was her ability to sense when I was in pain. She literally comforted me in some of my darkest hours. She snuggled up to me and placed her paw on my face as if she were caressing me. It calmed and comforted me in a way that's hard to explain. I just knew I was not alone and that she would always be there for me. I'd hoped to do the same for her, but always felt like I fell short...a guilt I held onto even today.

Life for Dandelion and me would have been perfect had it not been for one thing. Her little ear never stopped bothering her. I can't tell you how many visits to the vet we made only to get more drops, antibiotics, ear cleanings, and very high veterinary bills. But nothing worked, and she hated everything I was doing to her. Sometimes it got to a point where she knew what the medicine looked like, and she would hide under the bed…where I couldn't get to her. The dreaded drops actually stung her raw ear, and she would look at me like I was deliberately trying to hurt her. It wore me down physically and emotionally. My husband needed more and more attention and care as he became bedridden before we moved from an apartment to a house.

After five different veterinary offices, I found a woman who suspected something else was going on and asked if she could perform a biopsy. Two thousand dollars later, I received the results.

She had a small tumor in her ear that she suspected was cancerous. She removed what she could, but some remained. If it grew back, we would know if it was malignant. My heart all but broke, and I went home with my kitty, my best friend, and I knew I had an awful decision to make. The quality of all our lives had suffered because I had run myself ragged trying to be everything to everyone… my husband, my son, my grandchildren, my daughter, my kitty, and had nothing left to give anyone… especially myself.

My kitty was suffering, and I knew it. We were suffering together, and I had to be the strong one for her. I can't begin to explain how I struggled and cried and cried and cried until I had no more tears. She had been with me through some of the worst moments in my life. I may have saved her initially, but she saved me, too. We saved each other, and now it was time to say goodbye. I had promised her I would never abandon her, and now I had to break that promise. I handed her over to the people who, with one shot, would end her life. I did not go in with her… I couldn't do it. I couldn't look her in the eyes knowing I betrayed her… I abandoned her. I held her little paw through the cage and, choking back my heartbroken sobs, said goodbye. *"Goodbye, my sweet Dandelion."*

Chapter 7: The Day-to-Day

There is never a shortage of cliches when it comes to answers to questions such as, "How are you doing?" or "How's it going?" "Well, I'm just taking it one day at a time." That seems to be a common "go-to" answer, but it implies so much. To me, taking it one day at a time suggests we are just getting by or are a victim of our circumstances, taking us out of the picture, and absolving us of any responsibility, which can lead to depression, inaction, hopelessness, or helplessness.

However, we can look at our answer a little differently by saying, "I'm making it one day at a time," which suggests we are deliberately looking at each day as an opportunity. We are searching for solutions and are working toward improvement. Essentially, we are being proactive rather than reactive or inactive.

One is markedly easier than the other. With the first option, we sit back and watch our life go by as if watching a movie with a predetermined outcome. The latter gives us back our control and the ability to create options. Every day is a new day and a chance to make a change, no matter how small, we are contributing to an outcome, giving us a feeling of hope rather than dread. How we choose to look at a situation can make all the difference in helping us survive an untenable ordeal, giving us the fortitude and drive to forge ahead and to not only endure, but thrive.

I've become a believer in the phrase, "Attitude is Everything," because I have a husband who lived it every day. I know this is the reason he lasted as long as he did. I also know I would never have made it this far if I were in his shoes. I'm too much of a whiny-pants, and I would go crazy if I couldn't get out of bed for days or weeks at a time. But I was in awe of his attitude and his ability to make the most of his situation. He joked with everyone, telling them that he lived like a king. I guess that is one way to look at it, because I'm pretty sure I'd look at it in a completely different way, and it wouldn't sound as nice as that. Wait a minute, if he's a king, what does that make me? Again, it's all in the way you look at things, and even though my attitude was a bit skewed, my husband was there to remind me that life is what you make it.

As my husband's caregiver, I looked at every day as a challenge. The things I counted on to be the same were the only things I have control over, such as getting up in the morning at the same time and going through a routine every day, which only changed when something unexpected occurred. In other words, I'd come to expect the unexpected. Accepting this as part of my reality gave me back the power, preventing me from feeling a sense of trepidation and helplessness.

But that was when I was on top of things and taking time out for myself; otherwise, I'd be tired, grouchy, short-tempered and plain old grumpy. I'm not proud of that, but I cut myself some slack because I knew I was doing the best I could, and sometimes that's all we have to give. I've come to accept this aspect of who I am today, different from who I was before, but hopefully better.

Now, in all fairness, this took years and a lot of education, patience, and failure before I got to this place of acceptance. It's not the same for everyone, but the resources and tools are there if we take the time to seek them out. Going through this process is very similar to the five stages of death and dying (Elizabeth Kubler-Ross), which are denial, anger, bargaining, depression, and acceptance. Although I studied this in school, I didn't really understand what it meant until I went through this experience. It doesn't just relate to death and dying, but loss—loss of the person you once knew.

For instance, some Alzheimer's and dementia patients eventually lose their short and long-term memories, changing their characteristics and personalities. People I know who have family, or spouses that have one of these disorders, have told me they felt like they lost their loved one… the person they once knew was no longer there. This can be just as devastating as losing someone to death or sudden terminal illness.

In my case, neither of these things applied. My husband was my partner. We did everything together. I relied on him for certain things and vice versa. We also had a very active sex life that played a huge role in solidifying our relationship. It was literally part of who we were. But because he was bedridden, that part of our relationship changed dramatically.

Further, there were many things he could no longer do—things I relied on him to do (like anything construction-oriented). I had to learn to do everything myself, and those things I couldn't do, I asked for help, or I paid someone to do it, and I'm not talking about sex! I honestly never knew how much I didn't know how to do until I had to learn to do it myself. It's as if I had been placed in the middle of a football field with no gear, no training, facing an intimidating defensive line and told, "Okay, now go get a touchdown!" *What??!!*

It's not the same! It's no longer a partnership as in two people both contributing equally toward a specific goal. However, my husband adamantly disagreed. He believed we could still have a partnership, but on a limited basis. You see, his brain and memories were still intact. He was still in there, but he could no longer do the physical things he once did. Even the simplest of things—brushing teeth, using a lighter, pressing a button, combing his hair, and so on— were difficult, if not impossible. We had to make so many adjustments to accommodate those losses. One can only imagine how humiliating and frustrating that had to be, to rely on someone else for literally everything. But that's what he did, and with a great attitude to boot!

And sex? Well, I can't say we didn't try, but I was no spring chicken and definitely not as bendy as I used to be, especially climbing on top of a hospital bed, and trying who knows what acrobatics just to get into position…well, you know what I mean. I'm pretty sure my knees would have slipped off the sides of the bed, and that would have been a problem. It just wasn't feasible or comfortable, and pretty much all one-sided.

As for my husband, he gradually lost control over his lower extremities and was both incontinent and no longer able to have a bowel movement without help. So to say it was a challenge was an understatement. He lay there like a beached whale, with little or no ability to do anything to assist. In the beginning, I felt as if there had to be some way to mutually enjoy ourselves like we used to, but it soon became clear that it was physically improbable. First of all, it was extremely uncomfortable, and second, even with Viagra, the effects did not last, and it became apparent to both of us that we were going to have to be a hell of a lot more creative. Again, it just wasn't the same!!

My husband seemed to have a much harder time dealing with the reality of the situation, and for years, he blamed me as if I didn't care or love him anymore. He had everything tied up in our sex life and floundered under that cold, hard truth. It just wasn't physically feasible anymore, and that was a bitter pill to swallow for us both. We each processed this differently. I mourned the loss, and he got angry and made me the bad guy…for years. It took the better part of nine years before we were able to switch roles. He made peace with it and looked at our relationship from a completely different perspective. I, however, did not move on as I continued to have dreams that reminded me of how we used to be… always young, strong, and sexy… never with him in a medical bed or in his motorized wheelchair. It was pure torture for me, and when I awoke, I cried my eyes out, and my day started out with a deep sadness that lingered, reminding me of the harsh reality that was our life.

In reference to the five steps of death and dying... I was wallowing in sadness, and the fact that I was already predisposed to depression and on medication didn't make it any easier. I had used every tool and resource available to me to help pull me out of this quagmire and come to peace with it. It was shocking to me that after nine years, my feelings were still so raw.

All that said, don't lose hope; there was still intimacy, and touch played a major role in how that worked. Of course, it was still a bit one-sided as I had to initiate, but there were lots of little things that went a long way towards keeping the physical connection alive, and for men in particular, that was very important. Kissing, for instance, is a very intimate way of showing affection for one another. Yes, his lips still worked, and yes, you have to put in the extra effort, but the alternative is no physical connection at all, and believe me, it makes caregiving for a spouse ten times harder.

Now, when caring for a parent, grandparent, or child, touch is still vitally important for both the caregiver and the patient. I recall one particular study by American Psychologist, Harry Harlow. He conducted a series of studies with primates that really drove the point home. Using methods of isolation and maternal deprivation, Harlow showed the impact of contact comfort on primate development. In this particular study, infant rhesus monkeys were taken away from their mothers and raised in a laboratory setting, with some infants placed in separate cages away from their peers. In social isolation, the monkeys showed disturbed behavior, staring blankly, circling their cages, and engaging in self-mutilation. When the isolated infants were reintroduced to the group, they were unsure of how to interact—many stayed separate from the group, and some even died after refusing to eat.[6] Many similar studies have been conducted with primates, all ending with the same conclusion. Contact and touch are essential to life. The same is true for human beings.

In my case, I was so lonely. I slept in a big queen-sized bed all by myself. For over 45 years, I slept next to my husband, cuddled up close to him or in a spoon position, relishing the warmth and comfort his presence brought me. God, I missed that! On particularly lonely nights, I placed the other pillow behind me so it felt like someone was there. I remember when, instead of listening to his rhythmic breathing, I'd lie awake listening for any signs of distress, sometimes not sleeping at all.

---

[6] Association for Psychological Science, Harlow's Classic Studies Reveal the Importance of Maternal Contact, June 20, 2018

Part IV:

Burnout &

Survival

Chapter 8: Burnout

I used to think burnout was a workplace thing…you know, overworked and underpaid, boredom, monotony, stress, deadlines, long-term exposure to a toxic workplace environment, etc. I've experienced this, as I'm sure many of you have, but never to the extent of not showing up for work or having a mental breakdown. Caregiver burnout is different… There's a lot of guilt associated with it. Like any normal human being, the level of frustration and exhaustion can cause irrational thoughts toward the person being cared for. No matter how much you love them, there is only so much you can do; the rest is out of your control. It's normal to feel frustration and anger. It's part of the process when caring for someone who is terminal. For all the effort you put in… there is no happy ending, no light at the end of the tunnel. You are simply helping that person die comfortably for however long it takes… that is your job every day, with no exceptions. That is why asking for help is critical if you are to survive and stay healthy. However, asking for help is one of the hardest things to do, especially for me, a perfectionist. It's like admitting you are not strong enough to do the job. What's worse, asking for help means you are asking that person to take on what you are no longer able or willing to do.

A very dear friend of mine told me that when her husband was faced with a diagnosis of Alzheimer's, his family was quick to offer their help if ever needed. However, when the time came that she really needed help, there was always some excuse or reason why they couldn't help her out.

Knowing this and dealing with my own guilt and fear about asking for help, I found it extremely difficult to ask for it when I really needed it. But I knew I wouldn't make it if I didn't ask for help.

With great fear and trepidation, I called my son and daughter and asked them to meet me for lunch. I can only imagine what they were thinking, as I had never done that before. When they showed up, my heart was pounding so loud I thought everyone could hear it. Stifling my fear, I asked them how they were doing, how their job was, and exchanged pleasantries. Then, taking a deep breath, I told them why I had asked them there.

Gulp!

I started with some scary statistics and then what I had learned in a Caregivers Workshop. With tears in my eyes, I blurted out, "I need help!" As difficult as this was, I came prepared. I told them what specifically I needed from them. I said that I needed to get away at least twice a year for a few days. I told them to take turns visiting their dad on the weekends so I could go to the lapidary shop and make cabochons (something I enjoyed immensely).

Without hesitation, they both stepped up to the plate. Both, with busy lives of their own, knew the importance of what I was asking and didn't even question why. My daughter told me later on that she thought I was going to tell them I had cancer. She was very relieved to find out it was not what she thought and was more than happy to comply.

It had been two years since I asked them for help, and they both lived up to their promise. I was able to get away for a respite for days at a time, and they both visited their dad frequently on the weekends. I did a good job with those two! As frightened as I was to ask, I did it and was thankful and relieved. Don't be afraid to ask for help!

****

I knew I wasn't the only person to have burnout because many of the workshops I participated in dealt primarily with burnout and how to cope in a way that is healthy, albeit over-medicating seemed to be the go-to for most caregivers dealing with this affliction. Looking at the latest statistics on burnout among caregivers only confirmed this.

A study conducted by researchers from A Place For Mom, a non-profit organization that helps families find senior living and home care at no cost to the family, analyzed the latest available data, and here's what they found:

- Almost 42 million Americans have provided unpaid care to an adult over 50 in the last 12 months.
- 40% to 70% of family caregivers report clinical symptoms of depression.
- 23% of family caregivers report that caregiving has negatively

affected their physical health.

Caregivers, both paid and unpaid, are at risk of burnout due to the stressful demands of their duties. The Cleveland Clinic defines caregiver burnout as "a state of physical, emotional, and mental exhaustion."

Caregivers face an increased risk of developing additional health problems. According to Blue Cross Blue Shield's report on the impact of caregiving on 6.7 million of its subscribers, caregivers are at a higher risk for the following types of mental and physical health problems:

- Adjustment disorder (emotional or behavioral reactions to a life change)
- Anxiety
- Major depression
- Tobacco use disorder
- Obesity
- Hypertension[7]

When you do start exhibiting signs of burnout, you are typically the last one to know. It's usually the people around you who notice first. Don't get me wrong, these people love you and are concerned about you, but they really don't know the first thing about what you are going through unless they have been a caregiver themselves.

---

[7] Schier-Akamelu, 2023 Caregiver Burnout and Stress Statistics, A Place For Mom, June 13, 2023

Knowing this, I still get rankled when I hear, "You have to take care of yourself," or "You must make time for yourself."

Yeah right. I wish I could have found the time, or at least rationalized taking time for myself without feeling guilty.

However, I know it is critical to do that. If you have any of the above symptoms, it may be your body's way of telling you something is wrong, and it's time to evaluate the situation you're in and make some healthy changes. These are all coping mechanisms that, if left unchecked, can lead to more serious problems such as heart attacks, strokes, and cancer.

Knowing this, I learned to occasionally take a bath with perfumed bath salts and bubbles, or go shopping at Goodwill. I love that place! It gave me great joy to find hidden treasures for myself and for the grandkids. I also enjoyed working in the garage with my lapidary equipment, making cabochons and turning them into jewelry. I hope to open an Etsy shop to sell my jewelry one day, but I am procrastinating because I know I have to take pictures of everything and then price and post them on the website. Just thinking about it is daunting and certainly not as fun as making the jewelry.

I also enjoy writing and have written and illustrated two children's books for my grandchildren, which teach them life lessons and respect for the planet we live on, with the hope they will carry those lessons into adulthood. In reality, there's no shortage of things to do, but finding the time and energy to do them is still the challenge. I have to say, though, the one thing I will always have time for is taking care of our two grandchildren, which was and still is the greatest joy in my life right now. We only got them for a little while because of school, but when we did, we tried to make the most of their visit with us. I always had art projects or things that stimulated their imagination, but inevitably, they opted for video games or TV. No matter, we just loved having them.

The message I am trying to convey in this section is to try to carve out some time to do something you love to do or simply do something for yourself. Whether it's exercising, cooking, reading, hiking, knitting, or whatever, find that *something* that brings you joy and make time for it no matter what!

Chapter 9: Dementia

I just want to be clear, I don't have any direct experience caring for people with dementia, but I have taken many workshops on caregiving specifically for people with dementia. I also have second-hand experience with dementia patients through my brother-in-law, who had Parkinson's dementia, and my friend and neighbor's husband, who has Alzheimer's. Sadly, he has since passed.

My brother-in-law passed away last year, not from Parkinson's, but from physical symptoms associated with dementia, such as slow movements, muscle stiffness and tremors, and a shuffling walk. Something as simple as walking down stairs can cause the patient to misjudge their footing and fall. This was the case for my brother-in-law, and it resulted in a broken hip. His Parkinson's and dementia had already advanced, and his weakened condition would not tolerate hip surgery. A painful decision was made to avoid putting him through the trauma of surgery and let the disease take its natural course. Hospice was called in, and within a couple of days after his fall, he passed peacefully, with his family all around him.

However sad and painful as that was, it did not compare to the pain and emotional experience of living with someone with dementia. My sister-in-law spoke regularly about our similar circumstances, each so very difficult, yet so very different in nature. She told me about the delusions and hallucinations, and how he would talk to people who were not there, or think he had a job he had to get to, sometimes in the middle of the night. And then there were the angry outbursts, followed by deep depression that rankled my sister-in-law as she felt helpless to do anything to stop it. When turning to medications that were astronomically expensive, they did little to relieve the major symptoms, such as hallucinations that were all too real to her husband.

When I came to visit, I witnessed him choking (dysphagia) on his food (which scared me half to death), and struggling to talk with this slow and labored speech. He seemed to be living in a different reality, wavering back and forth from present to past or just being absent altogether.

To this day, I'm still not sure he knew who I was, although I had known him for almost 50 years. The only sign of recognition was a tear in his eye when I said goodbye to him. You see, we lived on opposite ends of California. My ability to come and visit relied on securing someone to care for my husband while I was away, and whether or not I could afford the cost associated with travel. So saying goodbye was very traumatic for me as I was never really sure if I would see him again. Turns out, it was last time. *Goodbye Uncle Joe.*

My sister-in-law told me the one thing she found the most difficult to bear was that the man she married, the man she knew and loved for over 50 years, the father of her children, was gone long before he actually passed. She felt like she was living with a stranger, which made caring for him so much more difficult. He didn't appreciate anything she did for him; he rejected meals, denied reality, argued about his delusions, and got angry when she tried to tell him that his hallucinations weren't real. Her exhaustion was due to sheer emotional stress. Her sleepless nights and utter frustration with her inability to prevent her husband from leaving the house made her experience seem absolutely intolerable, yet she did it for two years with absolutely no help.

****

In my friend's case, she had been dealing with her husband's intermittent symptoms of Alzheimer's disease for almost 10 years. Signs that something was wrong started out slowly. He began to lose interest in things they had once enjoyed before, he isolated from friends and family, he hid household items and then couldn't remember where he hid them, he started watching shows that were popular during his childhood, even the foods he had once loved became foreign to him and would confuse him. He would have angry outbursts when trying to dress himself or getting lost while walking the dog.

My friend worked in the healthcare industry as an LVN and could recognize things that many would not recognize as serious signs. Sure enough, after bringing him to a neurologist and after conducting several tests, he was diagnosed with Alzheimer's. As devastating as that news was, she already knew something was seriously wrong. She told me straight away that she had lost the man she had known and loved a long time ago.

The progression of this disease lasted longer than usual because he had been an attorney and was highly intelligent; therefore, he had more brain matter to lose. As a result, he lingered, and his symptoms came on incrementally. He seemed unaware of his deteriorating personality and gravitated toward sitting on the couch with his headphones on, watching reruns of Bonanza and The Andy Griffith Show. Because my friend had worked in the healthcare industry, she knew what to do and how to handle him, whereas most may have given up and shipped him off to a skilled nursing home.

This disease is insidious, and those who are caregivers suffer burnout regularly. My friend showed remarkable patience, and only when his symptoms began to affect him physically, when he was in danger of falling or hurting himself inadvertently, did she finally get help.

Unfortunately, the caregivers she's hired knew very little about dealing with Alzheimer's patients, and this, too, became a burden because they would allow him to do what he wanted even when she had carefully laid out instructions to the contrary. As time went on, her age, health, and emotional well-being limited her ability to care for him properly, and she had to make one of the toughest decisions she had ever made. She placed him in a residential care home where he would get 24/7 attention.

Unfortunately, she was unaware of the stress she was under, and even after he settled into his new surroundings, her blood pressure skyrocketed to dangerous levels, putting her at risk of heart failure or stroke. It took the better part of two weeks to get her blood pressure down to manageable levels. At that point, she knew she had made the right decision for both of them.

Here's the misnomer about care homes. Just because you admit your loved one to a residential care facility or nursing home does not mean you simply walk away from your responsibilities, oh no! Such was the case with my friend whose husband had Alzheimer's. Any time there was the slightest problem, my friend got a call. Most days, she was already there to ensure her husband made a smooth transition.

But the reality is, most caregivers at these facilities are undertrained when it comes to patients with some form of dementia. While the state requires CPR training, background checks, and TB tests for home health workers, they do not provide the type of training that covers anger management, handling hostile or violent patients, or passive intervention specifically with dementia patients. The state does require certification for CNAs and HCAs, in which they receive 8 to 10 weeks of basic patient care, including daily activities such as bathing, eating, dressing, meals, and hygiene.[8]

---

[8] Aging Care, How Does Staff in Long Term Care Handle Residents Who are Angry and Upset, June, 2021

Caregivers who only deal with basic patient care are not required by the state to be certified as a Home Health Care Aid and rarely receive adequate training when dealing with dementia patients.[9] So when a dementia patient becomes unruly, angry, or uncooperative during any of these activities, these untrained caregivers become scared, impatient, and frustrated at their inability to get the simplest tasks done, which in most cases, only exacerbates the situation. As a result, the patient's spouse or primary caregiver is called to come and help. These are the same facilities that charge upwards of $7,500 a month to care for your loved one!

In an article titled 'Inadequate Training in Nursing Homes' by an organization called Nursing Home Abuse, researchers noted that nursing homes have a responsibility to provide specialized care to elderly patients, but direct care of these patients is almost always performed by the most poorly trained workers in the industry.[10]

Patients are the ones who ultimately suffer as a result of inadequate training, even while nursing homes increase their own profitability by hiring and keeping poorly trained staff, stretching them to their limits, and paying them as little as possible.

- According to the Centers for Medicare and Medicaid Services, staff turnover in long-term care means patients do not get the

---

[9] California Healthline Daily Addition, January 5, 2015
[10] https://eldercareworkforce.org/education-training-meeting-the-needs-of-older-adults

benefit of direct care staff who are familiar with their specific needs.

- Staff who are untrained in behavioral or cognitive issues are more likely to abuse patients.

- Poorly trained staff are more likely to neglect important patient needs.

- Poorly trained staff may be unprepared for the challenges involved with direct care, resulting in high staff turnover, understaffing, and an increase in the odds of patients being abandoned.

- Poorly trained staff can cause harm due to their lack of knowledge.[11]

Trying to tap into as many sources as possible, I asked our part-time caregiver about her experience in dealing with dementia patients and what she felt was the most difficult aspect of caring for them. She said unequivocally, "Anger outbursts." She went on to describe patients who hit and threw things at her, only to forget it had ever happened just a short time later. None of it was their fault; they really had no control over their fleeting emotions, but it made caring for them that much more difficult and hazardous. What's worse, she never received higher pay or any training on how to deal with these patients and their angry outbursts. When working for an agency, she simply asked to be transferred to a different patient. Any training she had, she

---

[11] NursingHomesAbuse.org, 2024

pursued on her own in order to better her knowledge or to further her career options.

When researching this specific kind of caregiving, I noted a considerable absence of information on people who care for bedbound patients due to physical disabilities. I often wondered which was more difficult, caring for a dementia patient or one with physical limitations that require them to be bedbound. The funny thing is, when asking my friend (the one whose husband had Alzheimer's), each of us felt the other had it worse, but the reality is, they are all challenging, and for all the effort that goes into caring for them, the outcome is always the same. We are left grappling with the loss, guilt, and resulting toll it takes both physically and emotionally.

When I first started writing this book, I had not experienced that loss yet, and I could only hope I'd recover with grace and dignity without being a burden to my children. And I couldn't even think about it without tearing up. This man I cared for was my soulmate, my one love, my first love, and when he was gone, I was quite certain I'd never be the same.

Part V:

Closure &

Identity

Chapter 10: Going Back Home

Moving back to Sacramento almost felt like coming home. There was so much we missed. We did a lot of exploring in a place where everything was within an hour to two hours away. Both Lake Tahoe and San Francisco were about two hours away, Sonoma and Napa Valley were an hour away, and the local Sierra Foothill wineries (our new favorite place to go wine tasting) were even closer. Some of my favorite places, such as Bodega Bay and the Russian River Valley, were also an hour or so away, and I took full advantage of finding one beautiful Airbnb after another, exploring every quaint beach and river town along the way. If it hadn't been for the circumstances surrounding leaving there in the first place, it truly would have been wonderful to be back. However, there was still so much sadness that it was difficult to be joyful at our return.

We had lost our beautiful home in Elk Grove because we were victims of the housing bubble debacle. Not because of anything we did; we put down $ 95,000 and got a 30-year fixed mortgage. However, when I lost my job due to downsizing, the unemployment rate reached a record 11%, and we could no longer afford the mortgage unless I found a new job immediately. We needed both our incomes to stay in the black. No jobs were available for someone with a Master's in Human Behavior with four years of experience as a senior loan officer for both the State of California and a non-profit gap financing agency.

These permanent loans would replace construction loans; however, the construction industry was also at a standstill. Additionally, no one, I mean no one, was hiring, despite me having lots of connections. The competition was fierce because so many were in the same situation. You literally had to have a PhD to do the same job that would previously have only required a Master's or Bachelor's Degree.

To make matters worse, our bank refused to consider a loan modification twice, despite our flawless payment record. Under the advice of our realtor, we did a short sale. We opted for that in lieu of foreclosure because it would look better on our credit report. Within a matter of days, it sold to a couple who got it for half the price we had originally paid for it. I will never forget the devastation I felt when that couple showed up with a measuring tape to see where their furniture might fit. Just like I did when we first moved in. What a feeling! I remember it well. We were so excited. Now someone else was going to live in my beautiful home. "Farewell, Elk Grove."

All was not lost, or so we thought. We hung on by renting a home in Fair Oaks. The home was small and needed a lot of work, but we thought we were going to live there a long time, so we made several improvements. We painted, fixed drywall, installed a mirrored wall in the dining room, replaced the countertops in the kitchen, resurfaced the cabinets, replaced the old window coverings, and when we finished, it was lovely. It became our home. But the clincher was a guest house on the property where my son and his lady friend could live in privacy.

The yard was vast and covered with fruit trees, fragrant lilac bushes, roses and a secret garden with a swing. It even came with two wild chickens that my son's girlfriend named Jack and Hoodini (we really don't know why). They laid fresh eggs every morning, but we always had to search to find them as they were onto us and hid them every chance they got. We even had visits from wild turkeys that occasionally sat on our roof (how did they get up there anyway?).

Life was starting to feel good again.

We were there for approximately six months when my husband came home one day looking devastated. He had lost his job— something we did not see coming. Without his income, we could not pay the rent. It was the proverbial straw that broke the camel's back. We had no other choice, as my job search efforts did not produce a job that could save us. So we sold or gave away everything and moved back to San Diego with only a U-Haul truck's worth of stuff we needed to get by.

Unfortunately, our move back to San Diego was bittersweet. My husband, son and I were homeless for three months and stayed with a dear friend of mine while I looked for an apartment with no income except my unemployment, my husband's pension, and a healthy savings account.

I Am a Caregiver

Yeah, right!

No one wanted to talk to us. But somehow, someone was looking out for us because we found a woman willing to rent to us, and we were able to get a two-bedroom/two-bath apartment in La Mesa. Even better, my husband was able to get State Disability because of Peripheral Neuropathy after having four rounds of Chemotherapy that left him all but crippled. Pins and needles, he said, all over his hands and feet almost all the time.

Fortunately, I was receiving unemployment benefits while looking for a job, but job prospects were nowhere to be found as unemployment rates continued to break records. I was even willing to work for lower wages or part-time.

In total desperation, I started looking at jobs I had little to no experience in. I must have submitted over two hundred resumes, cover letters and a virtual dissertation of answers to supplemental questions. I produced a Vitae rather than a resume, just to highlight my experience in education, curriculum development for both Universities and High Schools, training and research development, including publication for Dr. B.F. Skinner's work on the Baby Box (Air Crib) and my follow-up work with his daughters. I had so many interviews only to come in second place, even with all my connections... It was slim pickin's.

My husband pounded the pavement too, but the construction industry was at a standstill, and virtually no one in his field was hiring. This went on for months as we subsisted on government assistance, of which we were both extremely thankful. We were able to pay our rent and feed our small family of three. That was all we really needed. We were happy.

My son's life improved as well, and because he was extremely adept at computers, he managed to find work at a computer tech repair company literally right down the street from our apartment and got to drive around in a cute little orange tech repair car. Striving for independence, he went from one job to the next, working his way up the ladder in the computer technology field until he landed a great job with a media company that provided mood music for department stores and headphones for fast food workers.

Things seemed to be going along smoothly until it wasn't. My husband's neuropathy got worse and limited his ability to walk long distances and wreaked havoc on his hands, which he relied on to do any kind of office job. Using a computer made up 75% of his job as an estimator and project manager. Plunking away at a keyboard, a couple of fingers at a time, significantly hampered his productivity, which was a critical component of his job. With the help of disability attorneys, a judge agreed with this assessment and awarded him Federal disability, which literally saved us.

However, I was not dealing well with the trauma of the last year and a half and suffered a mental breakdown. The prior year started with the passing of my biological father, then I lost my job and subsequently, our home. Next, my husband's youngest brother died of Colon Cancer, and while I was at the funeral, I received a call telling me that my dear friend in Elk Grove died tragically from a hit-and-run accident one block from her home. Then, my husband was fired from his job, and that's when we had to sell everything and move back to San Diego, where we were homeless for three months. In the background, while all this was going on, my son was suffering from bipolar disorder, the loss of a wife, a live-in girlfriend, and a job; he dropped out of college, and after attempting suicide twice, moved back home with us and started over.

My daughter moved to Washington, D.C., to work at a think-tank, which was a wonderful career opportunity for her, but I missed her terribly. Then I got the call no parent ever wants to get. My daughter was attacked in DC while walking home from work, just a half block from her apartment. She was traumatized, but fine. I, however, was not. I started abusing alcohol and marijuana. To top it all off, I could no longer afford my medication for depression because I had no health insurance, so my mood swings were off the charts, alienating both my son and husband. Hitting the bottom of the barrel, I went into a two-week rehab program and then moved in with my alcoholic mother and enabler father. What was I thinking?!!

I literally had no place to go but my parents' house, a place that traumatized me during my youth and continued to do so as an adult. But I didn't want to impose on my friends; they had already done so much, so with my tail tucked between my legs, I limped home to dear old mom and dad. I quickly learned how to avoid getting into unhealthy conversations when I returned from rehab.

My inebriated parents tried everything to suck me back into their dysfunctional world, pelting me with questions and giving me their unwanted advice. I simply told them I was tired and wanted to sleep. Fortunately, most of my time was spent in the rehabilitation program where I participated in support groups, and one-on-one counseling with both a therapist and a psychiatrist, who thankfully, prescribed medication for my depression, anxiety, and PTSD as long as I did not drink or smoke. Urine and blood tests were conducted at the beginning of each day to ensure that. I attended educational seminars, exercised, read as much literature as was available and started my journey back to good mental and physical health. This was my ticket to leading a normal life with my husband and son, something I wanted desperately. I knew it would not be easy, but I was determined.

One of the most valuable things I learned was setting goals for myself—realistic, achievable goals. I created a daily chart to track healthy habits and goals, and I also kept a journal. Writing has always been therapeutic for me. This journal was intended to track my dreams, interpret them and report back to my counselor. Dreams were a way to subconsciously process things I was unable to deal with in my life. They manifested themselves in the form of experiences I had no control of such as, earthquakes, forgetting combinations to my locker at school, not having studied for a test in class, trying to find privacy when going to the bathroom, not remembering where my class was at school, going back to school to earn a second Master's degree, but never getting one, and most frequently, the feeling of falling. All these dreams added up to a feeling of inadequacy and low self-worth. The lack of control had to do with my inability to ask for what I wanted for fear of rejection. It seemed so simple, yet these dreams continue to plague me even today, but in different forms. The only difference now is that I recognize them for what they are, and it serves as a warning or beacon for what's going on in my life that I might be unaware of or out of touch with.

Although knowing these things would seem helpful, I still find them frustrating and disturbing, as they often act as a precursor to how my day will go or what kind of mood I will be in. It's particularly troubling when I think I have overcome something, only to have a dream that reminds me that I have not. Thankfully, I have come to accept this as part of who I am, an imperfect human being, but one who continually tries to be better and, most importantly, content. Being restless by nature, I'm still working on being content.

The good news after all of this is that I moved back in with my husband and son, a new person (with the necessary medications) and with a much healthier outlook and disposition. I was back on my feet again and looking forward to a new life, on the road, the best time of my life!

Chapter 11: The Healthcare Epidemic

What has happened to our healthcare system in the United States? We are one of the richest nations in the world, and yet people in the United States experience the worst health outcomes overall of any high-income nation. Americans are more likely to die younger and from avoidable causes than residents of peer countries.[12] The statistics for aging patients with chronic illnesses such as diabetes, heart disease, cancer, Alzheimer's, dementia, etc., are even worse. Imagine being over 65 with a debilitating injury that is rare and has no prognosis or diagnosis recognized by health insurance agencies.

In other words, there is no protocol for people with physical limitations due to spinal cord or other injuries that leave patients bedbound. For instance, pain management, comfort care, hospice, and home care are extremely difficult to get approval for. Especially when it comes to prescribing needed medications such as Morphine. The Opiate epidemic and subsequent laws and regulations have all but tied the hands of physicians who order them for patients who really need them. Pharmacies in particular have placed ridiculous restrictions on

---

[12] OECD Health Statistics 2022

these medications in order to relinquish themselves from any liability. And the patients who really need them end up suffering as a result.

Bed-bound patients, in particular, have very few choices when it comes to care and garner very little attention unless there is an advocate working on their behalf. In this case, it was me, and it takes an inordinate amount of time and effort to get the attention of the appropriate health care providers before you can actually get the care you need. The real problem lies in the caregiver's ability to stay healthy enough to care for that individual, that is, mentally and physically. What happens when that caregiver gets older and is no longer able to do the things needed to care for the bedbound individual? What happens when they become sick or injured and need help themselves? Who do they call?

Well, there are skilled nursing homes and residential facilities if you can afford to pay upwards of $7,500 a month. Or you can pay a licensed caregiver to come to your home for a mere $45 to $50 an hour for 30 to 40 hours of care per week. Who pays for that? Unless you are independently wealthy or extremely poor, you do! The middle class is left footing the bill for this kind of care, as Medicare and most health care providers do not cover it. However, Medicare Part A covers skilled nursing facility (SNF) care for a limited time under certain conditions:

- Coverage: Medicare Part A covers up to 100 days of SNF care per benefit period.

- Cost: There is no cost for the first 20 days, $204 per day for days 21–100, and all costs for days 101 and beyond. Medicare Advantage Plan members may have copayments for the first 20 days.

- Conditions: Medicare Part A covers SNF care if you have a qualifying hospital stay, which is a medically necessary inpatient hospital stay of at least three consecutive days.

- Drug costs: Medicare Part A usually covers drug costs for SNF care.

- Nursing home care: Medicare Part A doesn't cover long-term or custodial care in a nursing home. Custodial care is care that helps people with activities of daily living, such as bathing, dressing, and eating.[13]

Now, if you are in a low-income bracket, you may be able to get Medi-Cal or Medicaid. Medicaid is a federal program and sets broad guidelines for the program, but each state runs its own program and has some flexibility in how it operates. Medicaid pays for nonmedical home care, such as help with activities of daily living, bathing, dressing, and transportation. Medicaid typically pays a home care agency directly, but it can also pay consumer-directed caregivers an hourly rate. Medi-Cal is a state-run program specific to California residents. While it does cover varying degrees of home health care, it does not

---

[13] www.medicare.gov

pay for long-term skilled care. In-home supportive services (IHSS) pay for individuals 65 and older who are living at home or have a disability. Of course, the extent of coverage is determined on a case-by-case basis. While Medi-Cal and IHSS provide partial or fully covered medical and non-medical at-home care for many aging adults in California, there are undoubtedly people who fall through the cracks.[14] I call it the dead zone…you make too much to qualify for these programs, but not enough to pay privately. That's where we are… the dead zone. I think they call that the middle class, and many of us Baby Boomers fall within that category.

There are no perfect answers or solutions to the problem of aging adults with disabilities in America. We just don't view this population the same way other countries do. Norway, Sweden, and Switzerland, for instance, have full pension and health care benefits for their elders well into their 80s. But it's not just healthcare provisions for the elderly; it has more to do with the culture of how we view our elders. For example, many Asian countries view caring for one's parents as the highest virtue, and elders are treated with the utmost respect and reverence. I believe we have to start there before we can begin to address the bigger issues surrounding our aging population.

---

[14] Institute on Aging - www.ioaging.org

Chapter 12: Ravages of the Bed-Bound Patient

My husband had been bed-bound for the better part of eight years. Prior to that, he used a walker and a wheelchair. We had hoped that he would progress from there, but the extent of his injury and subsequent surgery left him with a diminished spinal cord. It became painfully clear one morning, one and a half years after surgery, when he tried to get out of bed and his legs stopped working. An emergency trip to the ER and a CT Scan later, we learned that his spinal cord was deteriorating and had been reduced to a thin thread barely able to support body function. Everything went downhill from there, and what had once been considered a difficult life became a horrendous lifestyle change, which ultimately redefined our marriage.

Prior to moving to our new home in Woodland, we lived in an apartment that was smallish, so fitting a hospital bed, bedside tray, and a Hoyer lift in my living room was a bit of a challenge. I had no choice but to give in to the fact that my carefully selected decor would also consist of the latest rendition of Hospital furniture and equipment, which complemented absolutely nothing I already had in my living area. Needless to say, my hospital decor blended with a beach theme would never make the latest edition of Better Homes and Gardens.

That was one of many concessions we had to make in order to accommodate our new reality.

The next big shock came when we realized his wheelchair would not fit in the bathroom with the only shower. Talking with the property manager about a possible ADA Shower was fruitless, and there were no handicap accessible apartments available to rent. So, he went without a shower for two years. Instead, he got bed baths, which paled by comparison. Can you imagine not being able to fully rinse yourself off or immerse yourself in warm water for two solid years? It doesn't take long before you begin to feel grungy and smelly, no matter how many bed baths you get. It isn't the same!

Our new reality became the number one requirement when looking for a new home. It had to be spacious; the halls had to be wider than homes built before 2010; the bathroom had to be ADA compliant; there could not be any stairs; there had to be pavement or hard surfaces in the backyard so he could use his wheel chair to get around; the kitchen had to accommodate his electric wheelchair because he still enjoyed cooking; and the living area had to be big enough to fit a large hospital bed, Hoyer lift, rolling bedside tray, wheelchair and all his medical supplies because I didn't want to stick him in a bedroom, isolated from everyone and everything.

"ARE YOU KIDDING ME??!!" were the exact words coming from my realtor. I, of course, was confident it could be done.

I Am a Caregiver

What was I thinking? We looked, and looked, and toured many homes, some I really liked, only to find they did not meet the main requirements. Frustration and panic set in, and I had to make concessions (and little did we know, this was pre-COVID). We finally did find a home that was a veritable blank slate. The walls were white, the floors had dull gray carpeting, the kitchen and bathroom floors were a cheap gray and white patterned linoleum, and the backyard was nothing but grass and concrete with no real thought of design or landscape concept. But since it was built after 2010, it had an open room concept, the guest bath could easily be converted to meet ADA requirements, and there was a room between the bedrooms and main living area that would be perfect for my husband's hospital bed, Hoyer lift, rolling tray, and electric wheelchair. I knew I could make it work with a lot of imagination and with a significant financial investment.

My realtor was a shrewd negotiator and was able to knock the asking price down by $30,000. It was a buyer's market, thankfully. They accepted, and I went to work. Within three months, I had completely transformed that house into a beautiful home that could accommodate guests, grandkids, and my husband's many needs. I even transformed the backyard, tearing out all the grass, installing a patio cover and pavers that my husband's wheelchair could easily negotiate, and built a retaining wall out of pavers that served as a planter for colorful foliage and flowers. The finishing touch was an outdoor living room setting with a fireplace under the patio cover and BBQ, which was perfect for entertaining family and friends. I managed to accomplish this three months in early 2019 when the COVID-19 pandemic was just beginning. Just try to find subcontractors who are willing to go into your home and expose themselves. At times, I had to dress up like a mummy to either protect myself or the people working in my home.

The single best thing about this move was that my husband could finally take a shower! I think he took the longest shower he had ever taken. He told me later that it was glorious! All seemed well; we were making things work, and we had a routine. With the Hoyer lift (which a friend generously loaned us), an electric wheelchair, and the YoloBus for the disabled, we were able to go anywhere (within their route). We could go out to eat, we could go on a picnic, we could even visit our daughter, son-in-law, and grandchildren because she made her house wheelchair accessible with ramps. Life was good… until it wasn't.

Soon, it became all too clear that being bed-bound had many drawbacks. As my husband's fine motor skills began to diminish, so did much of his independence. Slowly but surely, he lost more and more control over his ability to roll himself from side to side, which was important so as not to encourage the development of the dreaded pressure wounds (bed sores). So as he got weaker, I had to be the one to roll him, hold things for him, and eventually help him have bowel movements. The more he lost, the more his needs increased. Eventually, our fun little outings became risky as my husband's jerky movements caused his electric wheelchair to swerve and jolt.

I Am a Caregiver

About five years ago, when my husband was still working out the maneuverability of an electric wheelchair, we took our grandson, who was three and a half years old, to a local park for a picnic. My husband seemed to be doing fine until he went to turn around, and, temporarily going off pavement, his wheels got stuck in the grass and he tipped over, with the full weight (300lbs) of his wheelchair landing on his leg and shoulder. This happened during the hottest part of the day, and he was quickly becoming nauseated as a result of sun exposure. Try as I might, I could not lift him, and while I was doing that, I was also trying to keep an eye on my grandson, who, fortunately, was playing joyfully with kids his age, and supervised by a mom who, seeing the commotion, voluntarily watched Hobie for me. So with no one there to help us but park maintenance workers who did not speak English and didn't know what to do, I had to call 911.

Fortunately, my grandson was not really aware of the seriousness of the situation with his Poppa, so when the firetruck and ambulance showed up, he was ecstatic and completely distracted. The rescue crew was top-notch. They created shade for my husband as they stood the wheelchair up, but it had died, and they couldn't move it. So, they manually pushed my husband all the way home, making sure he was safely back in his bed before they left. I couldn't thank them enough for their help and professionalism. My daughter and son-in-law came to get our grandson and to make sure my husband got back home safely as well. It was a frightening experience for us all, but we were just thankful there weren't any serious injuries, or so we thought.

Unfortunately, we wouldn't know until much later that he had fractured his arm when he fell and could not use it at all for what seemed like months. When we finally got him to the doctors, they did an Xray and sure enough, discovered a hairline fracture. With his weakened condition, he never really recovered and would not be able to use that arm in any helpful way ever again.

Just when we thought things couldn't get worse, he began to get bedsores or pressure wounds, because he could only lie on one side. I had never seen one before and had no desire to see one, but I did not have that luxury. I had to dress them, and these were mild cases. The wound specialist who eventually came to our home told us that pressure wounds can show up overnight and can become infected if not properly treated in time.

When they started showing up on his feet, they got worse in a ridiculously short period of time. The fear is that they go to the bone and become infected, which can cause death. WHAT??

And they expected me to dress the wound in between visits! Yeah right! That was not going to happen. *"I'm not a freakin' nurse! And by the way, I'm not getting paid for any of this!"* Okay, that was my rant, and I stuck to my guns.

The gal I eventually hired to be a part-time caregiver was more than happy to dress the wounds. Thank goodness! These wounds would continue to be a huge nuisance and required daily inspection and treatment. The worst part for my husband was having to roll to the side when the wounds on his rump hurt him. He could not do anything but lie there. However, the alternative was taking more morphine, which caused constipation. This was a no-win scenario and a constant battle. But, through it all, his attitude remained positive, which made everyone around him feel comfortable. That was probably the only reason he made it that far. While his attitude remained upbeat, mine went up and down, like a roller coaster of emotions, which was not helpful to anyone. I needed help. But this time, I needed therapeutic help, and I did everything I could to get it.

When my own health care provider failed to produce results, Hospice stepped up to the plate. I was able to get access to a Chaplain, should I need one, and a social worker. Both were readily available to me at my convenience. Sometimes, you just need to vent or talk to someone who will listen, and I had a lot to say. I needed someone who would really know what I was going through and who wouldn't give me anecdotes or canned responses and solutions, such as, "Have you tried this, or that?" Or, "Yeah, I went through that too and I did this…" It then becomes all about them and not you. I didn't want sympathy, I wanted empathy. There is a big difference. Empathy involves an emotional connection or the ability to step into that person's shoes and feel what they are feeling. Sympathy is more about a person feeling sorry or pity for you.

It's vitally important to note, the person you are caring for is not the only one going through this; you are, too, but we are all but forgotten because we are not the ones with the illness or injury.

And if you are not emotionally and physically prepared to do what is required, then you will both suffer. Someone who is bed-bound needs so much more attention than someone who can still walk or use a wheelchair. I compare it to caring for a quadriplegic patient. You have to do everything for them, and that takes a lot of patience, stamina, and a healthy attitude. No matter how much you love that person, you can still experience burnout if you are not getting the help you need or taking time for yourself.

Chapter 13: The Challenges of Caregiving

Just when you think being a caregiver can't be hard enough, something comes along that turns your world upside down and takes every bit of faith you ever had in human kindness and compassion and turns it on its head.

This happened to us, and after much research into this topic, it has happened to many others as well. I say "us" because I truly believe my husband was manipulated as well, whether he realized it or not.

There is an actual definition for Caregiver Scams put out by AARP. "Caregiver scams involve individuals exploiting the trust placed in them as caregivers to defraud or steal from their patients or their families. These scams can range from financial exploitation to emotional manipulation, with the caregiver often creating elaborate stories to gain access to funds or personal information."

Although we diligently tried to hire a caregiver through a certified agency, we could not afford the $40 per hour fee for a minimum of 4 hours a week. That was more than our mortgage! So we had no choice but to hire under the table, and believe me, there are many who are willing to do that as the agencies pay them a small percentage of what they bring in, usually around $15 per hour. We went through about three or four non-agency-affiliated caregivers until we found the one we liked, who actually worked for an agency but was willing to work under the table for us. We paid her $25 versus the $15 she was making with the Caregiving agency. She shined at first, especially for me and the light housework I asked her to do. But that faded, and she found a way to become my husband's friend and confidant. She was a master at finding things they had in common, such as movies, music, and pot. During her short stay with us, those things were always in play.

She would come in only twice a week for 2 1/2 hours to give him a shower and do some light housework, which she became terrible at. In his limited condition, he couldn't do anything. So she cleaned and lotioned every part of his body. She filled a role I no longer filled with the same freshness and enthusiasm, providing very intimate and personal care, where my approach seemed tired, impatient, and burned out after 10 years of providing it 24/7. Who wouldn't want that, and who was I to deny that level of care to the man I loved for 50 years?

But that wasn't her only strategy; she told us sad stories about her husband, who had mysterious illnesses that caused her to miss many Mondays and Fridays (the only days she came in), which we paid for without question. That's just the way we rolled. If we felt someone was less fortunate than us, well, we helped them if we could. Oh, and there were many misfortunes with mean family members, husbands being too sick and needing care, cars breaking down, family crises, etc.

Unfortunately, I had referred her to my friend, an LVN, across the street to care for her husband with early-stage Alzheimer's. At first, she was pleased, but soon she noticed the credit card she gave her for lunch and fun activities was going up exponentially, and despite my friend's best attempts at asking her not to spend it on fried and greasy food, she continually saw fast food restaurants with more food ordered than two could possibly eat. My friend assumed she was bringing food home to her husband and kids. My friend's husband gained 10lbs in three weeks! Then came art supplies and other purchases that just kept piling up. When my friend tried to ask her about the purchases, my caregiver told her that it was her husband's wish, and that's when my friend became suspicious. Her husband was not mentally capable of making any of those decisions, but was being manipulated by the caregiver I referred to her.

She let her go soon after, which is what I should have done. However, after having gone through so many and knowing each time there would be a training period, I figured I could keep things under control. After all, I didn't give her a credit card. What we did do to show our gratitude, came in the form of large Christmas bonuses ($500, $1,000, $1,500), large amounts of pot, paid holidays (time and a half), sick days, and any other days off, all of which we felt were acceptable rewards for her services. There were also gifts from me to her and the kids for Christmas, donated home goods, clothing, shoes, etc. I, too, bought into her plight. However, when mentioning this form of payment and gratitude to family and friends, they were shocked, alarmed, and anything but feeling like that was normal.

The alarm bells really went off prior to my husband's passing, when he withdrew $22,000 from our IRA without telling me. I think he told her she would get a large severance at Christmas, as he sensed he would not make it much past New Year's. As a result, I was strapped with a $6,000 tax bill, and things went downhill for me after that. It could have been worse. She could have somehow gotten that money, and I would still have been left with a tax bill. I had a nervous breakdown trying to unravel the mystery, dealing with the IRS, and bank errors that caused additional delinquent charges. Three and a half weeks later, I began to unravel this whole financial and scamming nightmare, and this chapter came to life. It also became part of my therapy.

I began by doing some research into this person who claimed to be a Licensed Family Therapist, Elementary School Teacher, a licensed caregiver, certified in wound care, physical therapy, and numerous other certifications. After doing some very rudimentary searching, I could find no evidence of any of these certifications or licenses listed on any of her social media pages. The woman couldn't put a sentence together at times, which should have been my first clue.

According to her social media pages, she displayed a wedding ring with a rather large Sapphire surrounded by diamonds, a trip to Tahoe in a very expensive honeymoon suite, a trip to Disneyland with her whole family, regularly got her hair and nails done, etc. She had revealed to my husband that former clients of hers had taken her on trips to Europe with them and so on.

But the one thing I did not see on her social media pages was stories about her family, her kids' accomplishments, her husband's trials and successes with his so-called mystery illness, her career ambitions, only rather suggestive and provocative pictures of her in various AI-manipulated poses. I felt totally duped and manipulated. Then, the unthinkable, I found a picture of her taking a selfie on my bed in my bedroom!

In hindsight, anyone you employ and allow to see your home in a nice neighborhood, with nice furnishings, is going to think that you probably have money, and that isn't always the case. No matter, that is the assumption. And because caregivers are paid so little for what they do, why not try to get as much as possible because they earned it, right?

I also didn't bother to check references. She was working for an agency, don't they do that? Check references no matter what! Ask to see credentials, certifications, and anything they claim to have. I didn't because frankly, I didn't believe her. I thought she was just trying to impress us, and I did not want to embarrass her. I didn't hire her for that, nor would I have. Don't let anyone in your house until you are thoroughly convinced they are on the up and up.

Not surprisingly, we were not the only victims of this sort of crime (scam). A 2019 review by the Federal Consumer Financial Protection Bureau of suspicious activity reports filed by financial institutions found that one in nine incidents of elder financial exploitation where the target knew the perpetrator were committed by non-family caregivers. The average loss in such cases was $57,800.[15] I guess we were lucky, but if my husband had actually been able to somehow get the money to her without me knowing, it would have been way worse.

Fortunately, the large sum of money withdrawn from our IRA did not go to our caregiver as "Severance pay," like my late husband called it. He passed away before I knew what was happening or what he was planning. I can only imagine what she said or did to elicit that sum of money, but he trusted and cared for her, so it was probably coming from a place of love and gratitude. Her motivation remains suspect.

Now that I look back at the reaction she had when we gave her the bonus check of $1,500 right before Christmas, it occurred to me that she looked shocked, not like before when she cried and said how thankful she was the year before when we only gave her $1,000. My husband must have promised her a check significantly larger than what we gave her, and the look on her face and tone of her voice were that of shock and disappointment. Whew!

****

---

[15] AARP, WatchDog Alerts, November, 9, 2021

As time went on, my husband's symptoms increased and decreased with amazing inconsistency. One day, he had nausea in the morning and was perfectly fine by dinner. However, one never knew if his appetite would return, which made planning dinner almost impossible. Then other days, the bed wounds caused him pain and discomfort, so we had to get him on his side, which left him virtually unable to do anything except lie there like a limp rag.

Other days dealt with severe constipation from the morphine he was on daily, and when I say severe, I mean two to three weeks at a time. When this happened, no amount of laxatives or stool softeners worked, so manual extraction was necessary to get things going. I wouldn't wish that on anyone. Believe me! Once that was done, it cleared the way for a deluge of backed-up excrement, which occurred three to four times a day, and each time, the procedure of changing bed pads, shirts, towels, and bandages took 10 to 15 minutes, depending on quantity and consistency. Let's just say it got real messy, and cleaning was arduous and nauseating, depending on your sensitivity to smell. I'd been known to retch if it was too early in the morning. This pattern would go on for days until we were caught up, and then we'd begin a regimen of Miralax and Metamucil once nightly to try and get things moving again. And it went on and on. So, my day began and ended with poop. Sometimes, when I went to bed, I'd think, *The only thing I have to look forward to is waking up to more poop!'* (an inner scream ensues, followed by self-pity and then guilt for thinking that way in the first place). It was a damn poopy life!

Let's not mention the astronomical cost of things like bed pads, butt pads, adult wipes, large band-aids, wound cleaners, barrier creams, diapers, suppositories, gloves, and over-the-counter drugs like Miralax and Metamucil! Ouch! We went through those things like water and paid for all those things ourselves. However, when we finally got Hospice, the level of care went up exponentially!

The reality is that no one really knows what's going to happen and when, not even the doctors. So a medical team came to my home and evaluated where my husband was in the progression of his deteriorated state and made a determination as to whether or not Hospice was required.

They had a set of criteria that included your ability to do things for yourself, the presence of pressure wounds, weight loss, etc. This process took months! Then we got Hospice, and they took care of everything! We had nurses for bed wound care, CNAs for bed baths, social workers for our sanity or insanity, and a Chaplain for our spiritual needs. All our meds were paid for and delivered to our home, which, up until then, required a trip to the pharmacy bi-weekly with hour-long waits to get his medications, mostly because they won't mail opiates. Hospice was wonderful because (and this sounds terrible) if you don't pass after six months, you can renew hospice care for another six months until you expire. Some patients, I'm told, have been in hospice for two or more years.

As with anything in life, when you think you're finally getting some relief, something unexpected comes along. COVID hit. During that time, my husband became incontinent. He literally could not tell when or if he was urinating or not. That was just one of many side effects associated with COVID-19, some turned into what they now refer to as Long COVID. When you heard that COVID can be a whole lot worse with patients who are compromised or have a pre-existing condition, they were absolutely right!

My husband and I both got COVID, but he got it far worse than me. At one point, we had to call 911 because my husband started having trouble breathing. After a very scary stint in the ER, the doctors informed me that my husband had Acute Respiratory Failure and had to stay in the hospital for four days. In a way, I was thankful because I knew he would get around-the-clock care. What I didn't know was that they pumped him up with a variety of medications, including steroids, which played a huge role in hampering his recovery and attitude.

When he did come home, he had oxygen tubes, tanks, and other monitoring apparatus, which made our already small room resemble an ER. His blood oxygen level had to be monitored, and his blood pressure had to be checked regularly. It was extremely low, and he had a slew of medications he needed to continue taking, including steroids, which altered his temperament significantly, and others that made him drowsy and nauseated. His horrible cough lasted for what seemed like forever, which made for many a sleepless night. For the first time in maybe 20 years, I had my mom's ears on, and unfortunately, I could hear every raspy breath.

This went on for the better part of three weeks, and after that, he was never the same. He lost many of his bodily functions, including fine motor skills in his hands, which made everything so much harder. We had to find new ways to compensate for the loss, and that became even more time-consuming than before. Things that were easy before became almost impossible. For instance, he could no longer use a lighter, he could no longer push buttons, he couldn't use a nasal spray, he couldn't open any type of container, and we mutually declared eating a major disaster area, and no amount of protection adequately prevented spillage or containment. All these changes required a new level of patience and tolerance, which I had in short supply. Much like a maid, I was at his beck and call, and I was the one who had to adjust; he still had his positive outlook, which, on some days, didn't sit well with me.

As I mentioned previously, my husband also became incontinent, and when that happened, we tried a variety of things designed to contain the flood of urine that he produced daily. We tried diapers first and realized he would sit in his own urine-soaked diaper all night long. He started getting rashes, and what we later learned was the onset of bed sores. So then we tried urinals, but unless they were somehow strapped on, they would inevitably leak during the night, resulting in the same situation—a smelly, urine-soaked bed pad and shirt. Finally, after advice from a variety of health care workers, we settled on a condom catheter, which required a urine bag that needed to be changed daily. This seemed to be a good choice at first, but I had to learn how to put one on, and that was a rude awakening! Let's just say Viagra helped make the job a little easier. This seemed great until I realized someone was going to have to do this when I went on a respite break. That embarrassing assignment fell to my son and daughter, who, bless their hearts, took it on with no complaints. Can you imagine? That had to be hard on both the patient and caregiver. I hated to ask them to watch their father when I was away because I knew what they would have to do. But we are all adults, and we all did what needed to be done. The responsibility also fell to the caregiver, who didn't seem to mind.

The biggest drawback to condom catheters, unbeknownst to us, was a susceptibility to urinary tract infections, which, of course, he started getting regularly. We had always heard that regular catheters, which needed to be inserted through the penis and into the bladder, had the biggest chance of getting urinary tract infections. But they are both likely to increase your chances of getting one, which becomes rather obvious after having used them. However, when he did get one, it was severe and needed immediate attention. All I can say is thank goodness he couldn't feel anything because he would have been in excruciating pain at the severity of them. I should know, I had them throughout my young adult life, and finally had to have surgery on my urethra. That is something I wouldn't want to go through again!

Ever since the onset of this condition, I became an expert at urine analysis. I checked for color (typically the color of dark tea), smell (sour), protein floaties or debris (which look like small flakes), foaminess, and foggy or cloudy urine, all signs of a urinary tract infection, which requires a urinalysis. In order to do a urinalysis, you had to get a clean lab sample. However, trying to get a sterile urine sample from someone who was incontinent was somewhat of a challenge. You could wait around with gloves and a sterile cup in hand, hoping he would know when he would urinate, or rush over quickly and hope to get the lid off the cup and get a sterile sample before he finished. But however you chose to gather it, you couldn't get antibiotics without that sample. Once you had the sample, you had to get it to the lab within 30 minutes. *Are you kidding me?* This was just another in a long line of adjustments we had to make.

As time went on, it became all too clear that his condition would never improve and would continue to diminish his already limited body functions. And who's to say what other challenge we may have had to take on? To say this prognosis was depressing was an understatement. But I had to remain strong for my husband's sake and try to put a good face on something we both knew did not have a happy ending. That is what caregiving was all about. Most of the time, there was no happy ending.

I have to say, though, the most frustrating aspect of caregiving was having someone, a guest, family member, or friend see what you are doing and think, "Gosh, that doesn't look so bad."

To which I would reply, "You're right. Now do it a million times!"

It's easy to see an aspect of caregiving and think it's easy, and anyone could do it. But when you do it day in and day out, it becomes a monotonous chore, which morphs into a burnout nightmare, and then resentment sets in as you realize that your life will never be your own ever again.

If you know someone who is a caregiver, don't judge them. Help them. Don't make promises you can't keep or have no intention of keeping. Don't say you're going to help unless you are really going to help. If you do these things, you will be rewarded with their overwhelming gratitude, respect, and friendship.

Part VI:

Legacy

Chapter 14: December 19, 2024

To say it was unexpected would be a lie. I knew this day would come. I just didn't think it would be so soon.

The day started like any other day, except my husband woke up feeling better than he had in over a week. He had just finished his round of antibiotics for a nasty lung infection and was finally feeling human again. His energy was back, and we shared our toast and coffee like any other morning. My daughter came over that morning with a present my husband wanted wrapped for Christmas. He was talkative and appeared to be in good spirits. It wasn't until our hospice nurse showed up to do a weekly check-up later that afternoon that things changed for the worst.

Prior to his visit, my husband and I had a heated conversation about using a real catheter. He hated the idea of it, and frankly, so did I, but the condom catheter simply wasn't working, and we had put it off for eight years. So when the hospice nurse showed up, he asked him if he had any experience in inserting them. It just so happened he had one in his car and had the experience with many of his patients. From the other room, I could hear the fear and concern in his voice, but he agreed to do it. I was relieved right up until the insertion, and I heard my husband groan in pain. Right then, I regretted it. I couldn't even come out to look at him because I knew how awful we both felt about it. I huddled in the other room, feeling guilty about the whole thing.

After the nurse left, he dozed off, but he awoke feeling nauseated. He called for me to grab a bowl, and I ran to the kitchen to grab one. Now, he had been nauseated before, and I always gave him some anti-nausea medication, but this time, he didn't want it. He began to wretch, but only clear fluid came out. I instinctively checked his urine bag, and it was about a quarter of the way full of dark brown blood. I freaked out and ran to call hospice. I didn't know what was happening, and all I could think of was the damn catheter. Had the nurse inserted it wrong? Was it too far up and punctured something? All kinds of terrible scenarios filled my mind. When I finally got through to hospice, they told me a nurse was a good hour and a half away. I raised hell because they are supposed to be available when needed, and they were needed.

By the time I got off the phone, my husband had stopped wretching but told me he needed the nebulizer because he was feeling short of breath. So I strapped it on and let it go until the fluid ran out. I asked him if he wanted Morphine, and he said yes. He was on an as-needed regimen with 1.5 mm of liquid Morphine administered every time he needed it. My cell phone rang, and it was Hospice telling me they were sending someone else who was closer. Relieved, I ran back into his room to tell him. But when I did, he looked gray, and he appeared to be in distress. I got up closer to him as his voice had gone, and the last words I heard were, "My diaphragm isn't working."

I could see he was struggling to breath and I instinctively pushed on his diaphragm, thinking that would help. When his eyes rolled back into his head, I started shaking his face to get him to come out of it, but he passed out. Panicked, I fumbled around for the phone with shaking hands, trying to call 911. I couldn't get through the first couple of times, and I was ranting and raving at the phone until I got through. "He can't breathe!" I screamed at the operator, who calmly asked for my address. I blurted it out, followed by saying, "I need an ambulance now, my husband can't breathe!" She calmly told me to calm down, someone was on the way, and suggested I start CPR, but there was no way to do that from the side of the bed, and climbing on top of him was out of the question as the bed was too narrow and I could never get enough leverage to do the compressions without slipping off.

The next few minutes were a blur as I ran outside to flag down the fire truck and ambulance. I think I was in a state of shock as I stood in front of my house crying and shouting, "Help him!" They got there as fast as humanly possible and immediately started administering oxygen, pumping air into his lungs with a balloon-like device and a mask over his nose and mouth. I continued crying uncontrollably while the paramedics pummeled me with questions, the most important being, *Where is his POLST?* I had no idea and ran around the house, tearing through files and drawers without any luck. While I was doing that, they placed a call to his doctor's office, and there was one on file.

It said DNR. Do not resuscitate.

I had forgotten that, and the paramedics asked me to make the hardest decision I had ever had to make. Just then, the hospice nurse arrived and was briefed by the paramedics as to his condition. They asked me if I wanted them to take him to the emergency (something I knew he hated and didn't want), with every possibility that he would pass before he got there, or let him die at home with family around him.

By this time, I was hysterical, and the paramedics tried to get me to calm down. They needed an answer, but I didn't want to give them one.

"Why can't he live?"

"Can't you wake him up?"

It was no use. What I didn't know was that his body was shutting down. It had finally worn out after eight years of being bedridden. He was going to die, and there was nothing I could do about it. Still hysterical, I called my son and daughter, screaming for them to come now. I was a snot-nosed, red-faced, tear-soaked mess and could barely stand without bending over in agony like I had been sucker punched. I had to decide before my kids got there. It became obvious there was nothing more they could do for him there. I knew what he wanted, so I told them to leave. My kids arrived just as they were gathering their equipment to go. I can only imagine the scene when they arrived, flashing lights, a fire truck, and an ambulance. The look on their faces told me everything.

The hospice nurse talked to my kids about his condition and told them I had opted for their father to stay where he was. Seeing his condition, they quickly went to his side and, gently touching his hand, told him they were there and they loved him. I huddled next to his bed and bent over, kissing his face and whispering that I loved him over and over again.

His breath was rattling and labored, but he did not appear to be in any distress. No matter, we were all crying and telling him we loved him as we waited for his last breath, which thankfully, came quickly. He must have known we were all there, because it wasn't ten minutes after they arrived that he passed. The hospice nurse leaned over and laid the stethoscope over his heart.

"He's gone," she whispered. We all looked at each other, and as if on cue, stood up and hugged each other, sobbing on each other's shoulders. After ten long years of suffering, it was over, and he was finally at peace. None of us would ever be the same.

Goodbye, my love!

****

December 19, 2024

The pain associated with grieving is something I didn't expect. My entire body hurt, and I felt like an empty shell, hollowed out and blackened with guilt, anger, sadness, and disbelief. The image of my beloved husband in his last moments of life left me traumatized. I have PTSD, and cannot seem to get that image out of my head. It haunts me daily, especially at night when I lie awake, eyes wide open, listening for him as if he were still there. An uncontrollable wave of agony racks my entire body, and my sobs leave me gasping for air.

There is no relief. There will never be any, as I come to the realization that I am alone now, a widow, and he is never coming back.

Strange how all the years of laborious caregiving fade away as I think about what I wouldn't give to have him back. I will miss him forever. I thank God every day that I got to have him for 50 years, 48 of those were in marriage. His remarkable attitude and our love kept him going where many would not have made it half as long. I am lucky and fortunate to be able to say he was the love of my life. I would gladly do it all again if I could only have my husband back.

Why?

Because I am devoted, I am resourceful, I am strong, and because I am a Caregiver.

****

"The goal in my life is to make those who come to visit feel better leaving than when they came."

~Bill Bailey

Resources

When I first started down this caregiving path, I was woefully uninformed and had no idea where to look or what to look for. Fortunately, my years in education and government taught me to be resourceful and to research everything. I became an expert at research, and with the internet as my primary tool, I was able to find all kinds of resources for caregivers. It doesn't take much to access these resources using a simple phrase—Resources for Caregivers. Boom! Starting with Federal Resources:

Department of Health and Human Services:

- Caregivers (MedlinePlus®)

Information for caregivers provided by the National Library of Medicine at NIH.

- Mental Health and Addiction Insurance Help

This consumer portal prototype is being released to help consumers get to the correct resource to solve their Mental Health and Substance Use Disorder insurance coverage issue.

- Proveedor de atención al paciente (MedlinePlus®)

Spanish-language information for caregivers provided by the National Library of Medicine at NIH.

- [Caregiving](#) (Medicare.gov)

Resources, stories, and newsletters about taking care of someone with Medicare.

- [Caregiving](#) (National Institute on Aging)

Information on caregiving from the National Institute on Aging at NIH.

- Caregivers (Administration for Community Living)

Help and resources for caregivers from the Administration for Community Living.

- [Alzheimers.gov](#)

The government's information resource for people taking care of those with Alzheimer's disease and related dementias.

- Eldercare Locator (Administration on Aging)

A public service connecting you to services for older adults and their families.[16]

State of California Resources:

https://www.caregivercalifornia.org/2020/10/15/can-i-get-paid-to-care-for-a-family-member/

---

[16] U.S. Department of Health and Human Services, Resources for Caregivers, April, 19, 2024

https://www.caregiver.org/resource/californias-caregiver-resource-centers/

https://www.dhcs.ca.gov/services/MH/Pages/AdultsCaregiverResourceCenters.aspx

Non-profit Caregiving Resources

https://www.agingcare.com/lp/bp-homecare

https://agewellseniorservices.org/wp-content/uploads/2020/12/CRC-Brochure-2020-ENG.pdf

*Del Oro Resource Service Center – https://www.deloro.org/ https://www.bigdayofgiving.org/organization/delorocares

This is just a sample of the online resources for Caregivers. Most of these sites will tell you what services are in your local area.

*Of all the resources out there, I found the Del Oro Resource Service Center the most helpful. They offer workshops on all areas of Caregiving, Respite grants, one-on-one counseling, and the most up-to-date information on Caregiving. They helped me immensely!

Bottom line, there are resources out there, and most can be very helpful. I encourage you to seek them out because there is strength in knowledge, and knowledge gives you power—power over your own life and how you choose to live it. There are so many out there in untenable situations, feeling so alone and powerless. Information and knowledge will undoubtedly confirm that you are not alone and that there is help. All you have to do is look!

Just a Note on Federal Resources:

I wrote about these resources prior to the presidential election, and given the current environment, I cannot be certain about the availability of Federal resources within the Department of Health and Human Services.

Positive, Comfort and Inspirational Phrases:

- Resilience: "It's not whether you get knocked down; it's whether you get up."

- Grief: "Grief is not a disorder, a disease or a sign of weakness."

- "Grief is the price we pay for love." E.A. Bucchianeri

- "Death leaves a heartache no one can heal, love leaves a memory no one can steal." From a headstone in Ireland

- Cherish the present: "After you have wept and grieved for your physical losses, cherish the functions and life you have left."

- "It is not the length of life, but the depth of life." Ralph Waldo Emerson

- "The most beautiful people we have known are those who have known defeat, known suffering, known struggle, known loss, and have found their way out of the depths. These persons have an appreciation, a sensitivity, and an understanding of life that fills them with compassion, gentleness, and a deep loving concern." Elisabeth Kübler-Ross

- "There are no goodbyes for us. Wherever you are, you will always be in my heart." Mahatma Gandhi

- "Like a bird singing in the rain, let grateful memories survive in time of sorrow." Robert Louis Stevenson

- "Be strong enough to stand alone, smart enough to know when you need help, and brave enough to ask for it." Ziad K. Abdelnour

I think that last one was my favorite. It reminds me of the Serenity Prayer, which may also be appropriate in this case.

"God, grant me the serenity to accept the things I cannot change, the courage to change the things I can, and the wisdom to know the difference."

Legislation

One key win for family caregivers was the passing of SB 616 (Gonzalez). SB 616, Paid Sick Days, expands the minimum number of paid sick days in California from 3 to 5 days. This means that all California employees, including working family caregivers and In-Home Support Service workers, will earn a minimum of five paid sick days a year starting January 1, 2024.

These sick days can be used when a caregiver or care recipient is ill or injured, or for either to seek medical diagnosis, treatment, or preventative care.

Among the other bills that passed this year that affect family caregivers and those in their care, as well as older adults in general, are the following:

- <u>SB 311</u> Medi-Cal Part A buy-in (Eggman)

Effective no later than January 2025, CA will be a Part A Buy-In state and simplify enrollment into premium Part A and the Qualified Medicare Savings Program at any time of the year. This change will help many individuals, but especially women and immigrants who do not have the work credits for free Part A.

- <u>SB 525</u> (Durazo) Minimum wage: health care workers

Creates a tiered phase-in of a $25/hour minimum wage for health care workers, including caregivers working in licensed skilled nursing facilities, residential care facilities for the elderly, and home health agencies.

- <u>AB 48</u> Nursing Facility Resident Informed Consent Protection Act (Aguiar-Curry)

Creates the Nursing Facility Resident Informed Consent Protection Act of 2023, which requires a prescriber, prior to prescribing a psychotherapeutic drug for a resident of a skilled nursing facility or intermediate care facility, to personally examine and obtain the informed written consent of the resident or the resident's representative.

- <u>AB 1309</u> Long-Term health care facilities: admission contracts (Reyes)

Requires nursing homes, within 48 hours of giving a required written notice of an involuntary transfer or discharge, to provide the resident with a copy of discharge related documents, including a description of specific needs that cannot be met and the facility's attempts to meet those needs when the basis of the transfer or discharge is because the resident's needs cannot be met in the facility.

- <u>AB 1417</u> Elder and dependent adult abuse: mandated reporting (Wood)

Requires mandated reporters to follow a single, simplified, and timely reporting process and ensure that criminal acts are reported to law enforcement first.

- <u>AB 386</u> California Right to Financial Privacy Act (Nguyen)

Improves financial abuse investigations by extending the time frame of accessible records from 30 days prior to and 30 days following the alleged illegal act to 90 days prior and 60 days after, which allows a thorough investigation to identify normal spending habits of the alleged victim. This bill also expands the information Adult Protective Services (APS) can receive to identify potentially critical evidence to uncover financial abuse. This includes: (1) new bank cards issued, (2) change of address requests, and (3) power of attorney.

- <u>AB 979</u> Long Term Care: Family Councils (Alvarez)

Modernizes existing family council laws so that members can meet and communicate electronically and continue to operate during a public health emergency. The bill also ensures that facilities will be more responsive to concerns raised by family councils, discourages operators from undermining family council activities, and clarifies that control of the family council membership and participation in meetings lies with the family council itself.

- <u>SB 544</u> Bagley-Keene Open Meeting Act: Teleconferencing (Laird)

Allows state bodies to hold meetings by teleconference with a member's remote participation if a member has a need related to a disability.

Vetoed or Two-Year Bills

Californians will have to wait longer for amendments to Paid Family Leave to make it "more accessible for chosen or extended family (<u>AB 518</u>) or available to multiple family members at a time (<u>AB 575</u>).

- <u>AB 575</u> (Papan) Governor <u>veto message</u>
- <u>AB 518</u> (Wicks) was held as a two-year bill, meaning it will be

continued in the 2024 legislative session

- Governor Newsom also vetoed AB 524-Wicks, which would have addressed caregiver discrimination in the workplace.

- AB 524 veto message

2023 was also a tough year for California Alzheimer's legislation. For a variety of reasons, none of the proposed Alzheimer's bills made it into law, with several bills stalled in the fiscal committee.[17]

---

[17] Caregiver Alliance, Caregiving Bills in the California 2023 Legislative Cycle, November 7, 2023

Epilogue

Two weeks before my husband passed away, he asked me what I wanted for Christmas. I wanted nothing except my husband back, but I knew I had to tell him something, so I asked him to write something for me. Not thinking anything would come of it, knowing how painfully difficult it was for him to write using two fingers with popsicle sticks and plastic condoms, I put it out of my mind. Christmas had taken on a whole different meaning for me, and what I did do, I did for the grandkids.

Ironically, the day he passed, my daughter stopped by with my gift. She had printed, framed, and wrapped it for him to place under the tree. He passed one week before Christmas, and on Christmas morning, there was only one gift left under the tree from him to me. My daughter didn't think I should open it so soon, but I needed to know what he wrote.

His last love story, poem, thoughts he wanted to convey to me... I ripped it open. Here's what he wrote:

"We already have the five greatest loves of the 20th century."

"Yeah, yeah. Some of these are obvious, Bogey and Bacall, Jimmy and Rosalind, Newman and Woodward, Wesley and Buttercup."

"Don't forget Diego Rivera and Frida Kahlo."

"A worthy list, but c'mon, Wesley and Buttercup? They are great loves, enduring loves, but they're not real. I want to submit Bill and Shelly instead."

"Actually, I have heard of them. They have instant credibility since people know them by only their first names, like Madonna. So consideration? OK. Certainly. How long together?"

"They've shared 49 Christmases. But their relationship has much more than longevity going for it. Do you know how innocent these two were when they met?"

"Only Babes?"

"Hardly even that."

"Well then, how did they survive that period of youthful volatility?"

"They channeled all their raging energy into a fast-paced rock and roll lifestyle."

"Certainly not an original attempt. That's a bronco ride that's been proven to end in disaster."

"Not in this case. After eight years, they decided to move, make babies, and build their own home!"

"After being party animals for long? Ha! Any one of those challenges can lead to divorce, but all three at once? Unsurvivable!"

"Not for them. They did all of it and more. They raised two kids, then moved to a new city and took on new jobs. But right after they moved, Bill got cancer. He survived, barely, but that took another two years to overcome."

"So they were dealt cancer along with their moving to new jobs? And they're still together?"

"More than just together, Bill used the experience to win a nationwide essay writing contest about how Shelly nursed him through cancer. They were rewarded with five days on the East Coast. Only a small payback, especially when compared to the life hurdle yet to come. After decades of fifty-hour work weeks, their retirement to an RV life lasted just three years. They hit a deer while traveling on a dark forest road, and Shelly became the main caregiver for the bedbound Bill. And has continued for the last ten years."

"Even that was not a deal breaker?"

"They have bonded even more. Because Shelly has attended to Bill's needs so diligently, he will soon complete a life-long dream of writing his autobiography."

"Hey, you convinced me! These two have gone from babe-like innocence through the joy of human intimacy, only to endure a hateful forge of repeated adversities and yet, emerged with an enduring love tempered beyond the touch of any corruption."

"They deserve that eternity on a warm tropical beach. We'll make sure it's reserved for them."

These were his last words to me, and I will treasure them forever... until, at last, we meet on those golden shores of a beach reserved just for us.

The End